"Is *That* Why Y[ou ...] Here?" She Asked, Watching Closely, Giving Him The Chance To Deny It.

"Depends," he said, cocking his head. "On what you mean by *that*."

"Because you thought I'd sleep with you?"

"It had crossed my mind," he admitted.

"You are the most egotistical, opportunistic—"

"Hey, you were the one who was dressed to kill and insisted on 'taking a ride in my jet plane.'"

"That *wasn't* a euphemism for sex."

"Really?" He looked genuinely surprised. "It usually is."

Amber compressed her lips. How had she been so naive? How could she have been so incredibly foolish? Royce wasn't some knight in shining armor. He was a charming, wealthy, well-groomed playboy.

Dear Reader,

Welcome to book number two in the MONTANA
MILLIONAIRES: THE RYDERS series from the
Silhouette Desire line. I love writing about siblings,
and I hope you enjoy reading Royce's story in
In Bed with the Wrangler along with his brother Jared
and his sister Stephanie's stories in the companion books.

The idea for this series goes back a long time. When I
was ten years old, my parents took me to visit my aunt
and uncle's ranch during the summer. Even at that young
age, I spun fanciful stories about the people living and
working on the cattle ranch. I thought the cowboys were
exotic and exciting, and I loved the space and isolation
that gave such a sense of community.

Montana is one of my favorite states, and since my
husband is a pilot, a cowboy and a business owner all
rolled into one, the stories came together quite naturally.

Happy reading!

Barbara

BARBARA DUNLOP

IN BED WITH THE WRANGLER

Published by Silhouette Books

America's Publisher of Contemporary Romance

 **SILHOUETTE BOOKS**

ISBN-13: 978-0-373-73016-2

Recycling programs
for this product may
not exist in your area.

IN BED WITH THE WRANGLER

Books by Barbara Dunlop

Silhouette Desire

Thunderbolt over Texas #1704
Marriage Terms #1741
The Billionaire's Bidding #1793
The Billionaire Who Bought Christmas #1836
Beauty and the Billionaire #1853
Marriage, Manhattan Style #1897
Transformed Into the Frenchman's Mistress #1929
*Seduction and the CEO #1996
*In Bed with the Wrangler #2003

*Montana Millionaires: The Ryders

BARBARA DUNLOP

writes romantic stories while curled up in a log cabin in Canada's far north, where bears outnumber people and it snows six months of the year. Fortunately, she has a brawny husband and two teenage children to haul firewood and clear the driveway while she sips cocoa and muses about her upcoming chapters. Barbara loves to hear from readers. You can contact her through her Web site at www.barbaradunlop.com.

For my husband.

One

Strains from the jazz band followed Royce Ryder as he strode across the carpeted promenade between the ballroom and the lobby lounge of the Chicago Ritz-Carlton Hotel. He tugged his bow tie loose, popping the top button on his white tuxedo shirt while inhaling a breath of relief. His brother, Jared, and his new sister-in-law, Melissa, were still dancing up a storm in the ballroom, goofy smiles beaming on their faces as they savored every single moment of their wedding reception.

But it had been a long night for Royce. He'd stood up for his brother, joked his way through an endless receiving line, then toasted the bride and the bridesmaids. He'd socialized, danced, eaten cake and even caught the garter—a reflexive action that had everything to do with his years as a first baseman in high school and college, and nothing whatsoever to do with his future matrimony prospects.

Now his duty was done, and it was time for a final night in the civilized surroundings of downtown Chicago before his sentence began in Montana. Okay, so managing the family ranch wasn't exactly hard labor in Alcatraz, but for a man who'd been piloting a jet plane around the world for the past three years, it was going to be a very long month.

It wasn't that he begrudged Jared his honeymoon. Quite the contrary, he was thrilled that his brother had fallen in love and married. And the better he got to know Melissa, the more he liked her. She was smart and sassy, and clearly devoted to both Jared and their younger sister, Stephanie. Royce wished the couple a fantastic, well-deserved trip to the South Pacific.

It was just bad luck that McQuestin, the family's Montana cattle ranch manager, had broken his leg in three places last week. McQuestin was down for the count. Stephanie was busy training her students for an important horse jumping competition. So Royce was it.

He slipped onto a padded bar stool, the majority of his focus on the selection of single malts on the mirrored, backlit shelf as he gave the woman next to him a passing glance. But he quickly did a double take, disregarding the liquor bottles and focusing on her. She was stunningly gorgeous: blond hair, dark-fringed blue eyes, flushed cheeks, wearing a shimmering, skintight, red-trimmed, gold dress that clung to every delectable curve. Her lips were bold red, and her perfectly manicured fingers were wrapped around a sculpted martini glass.

"What can I get for you?" asked the bartender,

dropping a coaster on the polished mahogany bar in front of Royce.

"Whatever she's having," said Royce without taking his gaze from the woman.

She turned to paste him with a back-off stare, her look of disdain making him wish he'd at least kept his tie done up. But a split second later, her expression mellowed.

"Vodka martini?" the waiter confirmed.

"Sure," said Royce.

"You were the best man," the woman stated, her voice husky-sexy in the quiet of the lounge.

"That I was," Royce agreed easily, more than willing to use tonight's official position to his advantage. "Royce Ryder. Brother of the groom. And you are?"

"Amber Hutton." She held out a feminine hand.

He took it in his. It was small, smooth, with delicate fingers and soft skin. His mind immediately turned to the things she could do to him with a hand like that.

"Tired of dancing?" he asked as the waiter set the martini in front of him. He assumed she would have had plenty of partners in the crowded ballroom.

"Not in the mood." Her fingers moved to the small plastic spear that held a trio of olives in her glass. She shot a brief glance behind her toward the promenade that led to the sparkling ballroom. Then she leaned closer to Royce. He met her halfway.

"Hiding out," she confided.

"From?" he prompted.

She hesitated. Then she shook her head. "Nothing important."

Royce didn't press. "Any way I can be of assistance?"

She arched a perfectly sculpted brow. "Don't hit on me."

"Ouch," he said, feigning a wounded ego.

That prompted a smile. "You did ask."

"I was expecting a different answer."

"I'll understand if you want to take off."

Royce gazed into her eyes for a long moment. Past her smile, he could see trouble lurking. Though women with trouble usually sent him running for the hills, he gave a mental shrug, breaking one of his own rules. "I don't want to take off."

"You one of those nice guys, Royce Ryder?"

"I am," he lied. "Good friend. Confidant. A regular boy next door."

"Funny, I wouldn't have guessed that about you."

"Ouch, again," he said softly, even though she was dead right. He'd never been any woman's good friend or confidant.

"You strike me as more of a playboy."

"Shows you how wrong you can be." He glanced away, taking a sip of the martini. Not a lot of taste to it.

"And you left the party because…"

"I wasn't in the mood for dancing, either," he admitted.

"Oh…" She let her tone turn the word into a question.

He swiveled on the stool so he was facing her. "I'm a jet pilot," he told her instead of explaining his mood. Time had proven it one of his more successful pickup lines. Sure, she'd asked him not to hit on her, but if, in the course of their conversation, she decided she was interested, well, he had no control over that, did he?

"For an airline?" she asked.

"For Ryder International. A corporate jet."

Her glass was empty, so he drained his own and signaled the bartender for another round.

"Getting me drunk won't work," she told him.

"Who says I'm getting you drunk? I'm drowning my own sorrows. I'm only including you to be polite."

She smiled again and seemed to relax. "You don't strike me as a man with sorrows, Mr. 'I'm a Jet Pilot' Best Man."

"Shows you how wrong you can be," he repeated. "I'm here celebrating my last night of freedom." He raised his skewer of olives to his mouth, sliding one off the end.

"Are you getting married, too?"

He nearly choked on the olive. "No."

"Going to jail?" she tried.

He resisted the temptation to nod. "Going to Montana."

She smiled at his answer. "There's something wrong with Montana?"

"There is when you were planning to be in Dubai and Monaco."

Her voice turned melodic, and she shook her head in mock sympathy. "You poor, poor man."

He grunted his agreement. "I'll be babysitting the family ranch. Our manager broke his leg, and Jared's off on his honeymoon."

Her smile stayed in place, but something in her eyes softened. "So, you really are a nice guy?"

"A regular knight in shining armor."

"I like that," she said. Then she was silent for a moment, tracing a swirl in the condensation on the full glass in front of her. "There are definitely times when a girl could use a knight in shining armor."

Royce heard the catch in her voice and saw the tightness in her profile. The trouble was back in her expression.

"This one of those times?" he found himself asking, even though he knew better.

She propped an elbow on the polished bar and leaned her head against her hand, facing him. "Have you ever been in love, Royce Ryder?"

"I have not," he stated without hesitation. And he didn't ever intend to go there. Love guaranteed nothing and complicated everything.

"Don't you think Melissa looked happy today?"

"I'm guessing most brides are happy."

"They are," Amber agreed. Then she lifted her head and moved her left hand, and he realized he'd missed the three carats sparkling on the third finger.

Rookie mistake. What the hell was the matter with him tonight?

Amber should have had more sense than to attend a wedding in her current mood. She should have made up an obligation or faked a headache. Her mother was in New York for the weekend, but it wasn't as if her father needed moral support at a social function.

"You're engaged." Royce Ryder's voice pierced her thoughts, his gaze focused on her ring.

"I am," she admitted, reflexively twisting the diamond in a circle around her finger.

"Don't I feel stupid," Royce muttered.

She cocked her head, and their gazes met and held.

"Why?" she asked.

He gave a dry chuckle and raised his martini glass to

his lips. "Because I may be subtle, but I *am* hitting on you."

She fought a grin at his bald honesty. "Sorry to disappoint you."

"Not your fault."

True. She had been up-front with him. Still, she couldn't help wondering if there was something in her expression, her tone of voice, or maybe her body language that had transmitted more than a passing interest. Not that she'd cheat on Hargrove. Even if...

She shut those thoughts down.

She'd never cheat on Hargrove. But there was no denying that Royce was an incredibly attractive man. He seemed smart. He had a good sense of humor. If she was the type to get picked up, and if he was the one doing the picking, and if she wasn't engaged, she might just be interested.

"What?" he prompted, scanning her expression.

"Nothing." She turned back to her drink. "I'll understand if you leave."

He shifted, and his tone went low. "I'll understand if you ask me to go."

Her brain told her mouth to form the words, but somehow they didn't come out. A few beats went by while the bartender served another couple at the end of the bar, a smoky tune vibrated from the ballroom and a group of young women laughed and chatted as they pulled two tables together in the center of the lounge.

"He here?" asked Royce, cutting a glance to the ballroom. "Did you have a fight?"

Amber shook her head. "He's in Switzerland."

Royce straightened. "Ahh."

"What ahh?"

His deep, blue-eyed gaze turned cocky and speculative. "You're lonely."

Amber's mouth worked in silence for an outraged second. "I am *not* lonely. At least not that way. I'm here with my father."

"What way, then?"

"What way what?" She stabbed the row of olives up and down in her drink.

"In what way are you lonely?"

Why on earth had she put it that way? What was wrong with her? "I am not lonely at all."

"Okay."

"I'm…" She struggled to sort out her feelings.

In a very real way, she *was* lonely. She couldn't talk to her parents. She sure as heck couldn't talk to Hargrove. She couldn't even talk to her best friend, Katie.

Katie was going to be the maid of honor at Amber's wedding next month. They'd bought the bridesmaid dress in Paris. Oriental silk. Flaming orange, which sounded ridiculous, but was interspersed with gold and midnight plum, and looked fabulous on Katie's delicate frame.

Hargrove Alston was the catch of the city. And it wasn't as if there was anything wrong with him. At thirty-three, he was already a partner in one of Chicago's most prestigious law firms. He had a venerated family, impeccable community and political connections. If everything went according to plan, he'd be running for the U.S. Senate next year.

She really had no cause for complaint.

It wasn't as if the sex was bad. It was perfectly, well, pleasant. So was Hargrove. He was a decent and pleasant man. Not every woman could say that about her future husband.

She downed the rest of her martini, hoping it would ease the knot of tension that had stubbornly cramped her stomach for the past month.

Royce signaled the bartender for another round, and she let him.

He polished off his own drink while the bartender shook a mixture of ice and Gray Goose that clattered against the frosted silver shaker. Then the man produced two fresh glasses and strained the martinis.

"His name is Hargrove Alston," she found herself telling Royce.

Royce gave a nod of thanks to the man and lifted both glasses. "Shall we find a table?"

The suggestion startled Amber. She gave a guilty glance around the lounge, feeling like an unfaithful barfly. But nobody was paying the slightest bit of attention to them.

She'd started dating Hargrove when she was eighteen, so she'd never taken up with a stranger in a bar. Not that Royce was a stranger. He was the best man, brother of her father's business associate. It was a completely different thing than encouraging a stranger.

She slipped off the bar stool. "Sure."

At a quiet, corner table, Royce set their drinks down. He pulled one of the padded armchairs out for her, and she eased into the smooth, burgundy leather, crossing her legs and tugging her gold dress to midthigh.

"Hargrove Alston?" he asked as he took the seat opposite, moving the tiny table lamp to one side so their view of each other was unobstructed.

"He's going to run for the U.S. Senate."

"You're marrying a politician?"

"Not necessarily—" She cut herself short. Wow. How

had *that* turned into real words? "I mean, he hasn't been elected yet," she quickly qualified.

"And what do you do?" asked Royce.

Amber pursed her lips and lifted the fresh drink. "Nothing."

"Nothing?"

She shook her head. It was, sadly, the truth. "I graduated University of Chicago," she offered.

"Fine Arts?" he asked.

"Public Administration. An honors degree." It had seemed like a good idea, given Hargrove's political aspirations. At least she'd be in a position to understand the complexities of his work.

"You've got my attention," said Royce, with a look of admiration.

"Only just now?" she joked. But the moment the words were out, she realized what she'd done. She was flirting with Royce.

His blue eyes twinkled with awareness. Then they darkened and simmered. He eased forward. "Amber, you had my attention the second I laid eyes on you."

She stilled, savoring the sound of her name, wrapping her mind around his words as a dangerous warmth sizzled up inside her. The rest of the room disappeared as seconds ticked by, while he waited for her response.

Then his smiled softened, and the predatory gleam went out of his eyes. "I take it that was an accident?"

"I'm not sure," she admitted.

"Well, let me know when you decide."

If flirting with him wasn't an accident, it was definitely a mistake. She needed to get herself back under control. "Tell me about Montana," she tried. "I've never been there."

He drew back, tilting his head to one side for a second, then obviously deciding to let her off the hook. "What do you want to know?"

"Your ranch," she rushed on. "Tell me about your ranch."

"We have cattle."

A cocktail waitress set a small bowl of mixed nuts on the table and took note of their drink levels as Royce thanked her.

"How many?" asked Amber as the woman strode away.

"Around fifty thousand head."

"That's a lot of cows to babysit."

"Tell me about it."

"Horses?" she prompted, determined to keep the conversation innocuous.

"Hundreds."

She plucked an almond from the clear bowl. "I took dressage lessons when I was eleven."

His wide smile revealed straight, white teeth. "In Chicago?"

"Birmingham Stables." She nibbled on the end of the nut. "I didn't last long. I wasn't crazy about sweat and manure."

"You'd hate Montana."

"Maybe not. Tell me something else about it."

"My sister has a horse ranch up in the hills. It has huge meadows with millions of wildflowers."

"Wildflowers are nice." Amber was pretty sure she'd like fields of wildflowers. "What else?"

"She jumps Hanoverians."

"Really? Is she good?"

"We expect her to make the next Olympic team."

"I bet she loves it." Amber tried to imagine what it would be like to be so passionate about something that you were one of the best in the world.

Royce nodded. "Ever since she was five." The glow in his eyes showed his pride in his sister.

Amber sighed and took a second almond. "I wish I loved something."

He considered her words for a few seconds. "Everybody loves something."

She dared to meet his eyes and rest there. "What do you love?"

He didn't hesitate. "Going Mach 1 in a Gulfstream. On a clear night. Over the Nevada desert."

"Get to do it often?"

"Not often enough."

Amber couldn't help but smile. "Are you good?"

His gaze flicked to the low neckline of her dress as his voice turned to a rumble. "I am very, very good."

"You are very, very bad," she countered, with a waggle of her finger.

He grinned unrepentantly, and the warmth sizzled up inside her all over again.

"Your turn," he told her.

She didn't understand.

"What do you love?"

Now, there was a question.

She bought herself some time by taking a sip of her drink.

"Designer shoes," she decided, setting the long-stemmed glass back down on the table.

He leaned sideways to peer under the table. "Liar."

"What do you mean?" She stretched out a leg to show off her black, stiletto sandals.

"I've dated women with a shoe fetish."

"I never said I had a fetish."

"Yours are unpretentious." Before she knew it, he'd scooped her foot onto his knee. "And there's a frayed spot on the strap." His thumb brushed her ankle as he gestured. "You've worn them more than twice."

"I didn't say I was extravagant about it." She desperately tried to ignore the warmth of his hand, but her pulse had jumped, and she could feel moisture forming at her hairline.

"Try again," he told her.

"Birthday cake." She was more honest this time. "Three layers with sickly, sugary buttercream icing and bright pink rosebuds."

He laughed and set her foot back on the floor.

Thank goodness.

"How old are you?" he asked, scooping a handful of nuts.

"Twenty-two. You?"

"Thirty-three."

"Seriously?"

"Yeah. Why?"

She shrugged, hesitated, then plunged in. "Hargrove is thirty-three, and he seems a lot older than you."

"That's because I'm a pilot—daring and carefree. He's a politician—staid and uptight. No comparison, really."

"You've never even met him." Yet the analysis was frighteningly accurate.

Royce's expression turned serious. "Why are you hiding out?"

"What?"

"When I first saw you over at the bar, you said you were hiding out. From what?"

What, indeed.

Amber took a deep breath, smoothing both palms in parallel over her hair. She scrunched her eyes shut for a long moment.

She was hiding out from the glowing bride, the happy guests and the pervasive joy of happily-ever-after.

But even as she rolled the explanation around, she knew it wasn't right. She didn't begrudge Melissa her happiness.

Truth was, she was hiding out from herself, from the notion that she was living a lie, from the realization that she'd wrapped her life around a man she didn't love.

The truth was both frightening and exhausting, and she needed time to figure it all out. More than an evening. More than a day. Even more than a weekend.

She needed to come to terms with the colossal mess she'd made of her life and decide where to go next. Ironic, really. Where Royce dreaded his ranch in Montana, she'd give anything—

Her eyes popped open, and she blinked him into focus. "Take me with you."

His brow furrowed. "What?"

"Take me with you to Montana." Nobody would look for her in Montana. She'd be free of dress fittings and florists and calligraphers. No more gift registries or parties or travel agents.

No more Hargrove.

The thought took a weight off her shoulders, and the knot in her stomach broke free. Not good.

"Are you joking?" asked Royce.

"No."

"Are you crazy?"

"Maybe." Was she crazy? This certainly felt insane. Unfortunately, it also felt frighteningly right.

"I'm not taking an engaged woman with me to Montana."

"Why not?"

He held out his palms, gesturing in the general vicinity of her neckline and the rest of her dress. "Because... Because... Well, because your fiancé would kill me, for one."

"I won't tell him."

"Right. That plan always ends well."

"I'm serious. He'll never know."

"Forget it."

No. She wouldn't forget it. This was the first idea in weeks that had felt right to her.

She pulled off her diamond ring, setting it on the table between them. "There. No more fiancé. No more problem."

"It doesn't have to be on your finger to count."

"Yeah?" she challenged.

"Yeah," he confirmed.

"What if I wasn't engaged?" Her words cut to absolute silence between them. The other sounds in the room muted, and time slowed down.

His gaze took a methodical trip from her cleavage to her waist, then backtracked to her eyes. "Sweetheart, if you weren't engaged, I'd say fasten your seat belt."

She snapped open her handbag. "Then how about this?" Retrieving her slim, silver cell phone, she typed a quick message and handed it over to Royce.

He squinted in the dim light, brows going up as he read the typed words.

I'm so sorry. I can't marry you. I need some time to think.

"Press Send," she told him. "Press Send, and take me to Montana."

"*There you are,* pumpkin." Amber's father stepped up behind her, and his broad hand came down on her shoulder.

Shock rushed straight from her brain all the way to her toes. She whipped her head around to look up. "Daddy?"

"The limo's at the curb." Her father's glance went to Royce.

Royce placed the cell phone facedown on the table and stood up to hold out his hand. "Royce Ryder. Jared's brother."

Her father shook. "David Hutton. We met briefly in the receiving line."

"Good to see you again, sir."

"You've been entertaining my daughter?"

"The other way around," said Royce, his gaze going to Amber. "She's an interesting woman. You must be proud."

Her father gave her shoulder a squeeze. "We certainly are. But it's getting late, honey. We need to get home."

No, Amber wanted to yell. She didn't want to go home. She wanted to stay here with Royce and completely change her life. She wanted to break it off with Hargrove and escape to Montana. She truly did.

Royce picked up the phone and slipped it back into her purse, clicking the purse shut with finality then handing it to her. "It was fun meeting you."

Amber opened her mouth, but no words came out.

Her father scooped a hand under her elbow and gently urged her to her feet.

She stared at Royce, trying to convey her desperation, hoping he'd understand the look in her eyes and do something to help her. But he didn't. And her father took a step, and she took a step. And another, and another.

"Amber?" Royce called, and relief shot though her. He knew. He understood. He was coming to her rescue.

But when she turned, he was holding out her engagement ring.

"Amber," her father admonished, shock clear in his tone.

"My hands were swelling," she answered lamely.

Royce didn't bother making eye contact as he dropped the diamond into the palm of her hand.

Two

"Who was that?" Stephanie's voice startled Royce as he watched Amber exit the lounge on her father's arm.

Tearing his eyes from the supple figure beneath the gold-and-red dress, he turned to face his sister. Stephanie looked young and unusually feminine in her ice-pink, strapless, satin bridesmaid dress. It had a full, flowing, knee-length skirt and a wide, white sash that matched her dangling, satin-bead earrings.

"Are all women crazy?" he asked, trying to recall the last time he'd seen Stephanie in anything other than riding clothes.

"Yes, we are," she answered without hesitation, linking her arm with his. "So you probably don't want to upset us. Like, for example, turning down our perfectly reasonable requests."

Royce sighed, steering her back to the table as he

pushed the bizarre conversation with Amber out of his mind. "What do you want, Steph?"

"A million dollars."

"No."

"Hey," she said, sliding into Amber's vacated seat as the cocktail waitress removed the empty martini glass. She kicked off one sandal and tucked her ankle under the opposite thigh on the roomy chair. "I'm a woman on the edge here."

"On the edge of what?" He pushed his half-full drink away. Had Amber's text message been an elaborate joke? If so, how warped was her sense of humor?

"Sanity," said Stephanie. "There's this stallion in London."

"Talk to Jared." Royce wasn't getting caught up in his sister's insatiable demands for her jumping stable.

"It's Jared's wedding night. He already went upstairs. You're in charge now."

Royce glanced at his watch. "And you think I'm a soft touch?"

"You always have been in the past."

"Forget it."

"His name's Blanchard's Run."

"I said forget it." He had time for maybe four hours of sleep before he had to get to the airport and preflight the jet.

"But—" Stephanie suddenly stopped, blinking in surprise as she glanced above his head.

"I sent it," came a breathless voice that Royce already easily recognized.

He jerked his head around to confirm it was Amber.

"Sent what?" asked Stephanie.

Amber's jewel-blue eyes were shining with a mixture of trepidation and excitement.

She hadn't.

She wouldn't.

"Where's your father?" asked Royce. Was this another warped joke?

"He left. I told him to send the limo back for me later."

Royce shook his head, refusing to believe any woman would do something that impulsive. "You did not send it."

But Amber nodded, then she glanced furtively around the lounge. "I figure I have about ten minutes to get out of here."

"What did you send?" Stephanie demanded. "To *who?*"

Amber slipped into the vacant third seat between them and leaned forward, lowering her voice. "I broke off my engagement."

Stephanie looked both shocked and excited. She reached for Amber's hand and squeezed it. "With *who?*"

"Hargrove Alston."

"The guy who's going to run for the Senate?"

Royce stared at his sister in astonishment.

"I read it in *People,*" she told him with a dismissive wave of her hand. Then she turned her attention back to Amber. "Is he mad? Is he after you now?"

"He's in Switzerland."

"Then you're safe."

"Not for long. As soon as Hargrove reads my text, he'll call my dad, and my dad will turn the limo around."

Stephanie's lips pursed into an O of concern, and her breath whooshed out.

Amber nodded her agreement, and both women turned expectantly to Royce.

"What?"

"We have to go," said Stephanie, her expression hinting that he was a little slow on the uptake.

"To Montana," Amber elaborated.

"Now," said Stephanie with a nod of urgency.

"They'll never think to look for me in Montana," Amber elaborated.

"I'm not taking you to—"

But Stephanie jumped up from her chair. "To the airport," she declared in a ridiculously dramatic tone.

"Right." Amber nodded, rising, as well, smoothing her sexy dress over her hips as she stood on her high heels.

"Stop," Royce demanded, and even the laughing women at the table next to them stopped talking and glanced over.

"Shh," Stephanie hissed.

Royce lowered his voice. "We are *not* rushing off to the airport like a bunch of criminals."

Stephanie planted both hands on the tabletop. "And why not?"

"Six minutes," Amber helpfully informed them.

He shot her a look of frustration. "Don't be such a wimp. If he yells at you, he yells at you."

Amber's brows rose. "I'm not afraid he'll yell at me."

"Then, what's the problem?"

"I'm afraid he'll talk me out of it."

"That's ridiculous. You're a grown woman. It's your life."

"It is," Amber agreed. "And I want to come to Montana."

The look she gave him was frank and very adult. Perhaps his first instinct had been right. Maybe there was something between them. Maybe he was the reason she'd made the decision to finally dump the loser fiancé and move on.

He felt a rush of pride, a hit of testosterone and, quite frankly, the throb of arousal. Having Amber around would definitely make Montana more palatable. Only a fool would put barriers in her way.

He stood and tossed a couple of twenties on the table. "The airport, then."

Since he'd had the martinis, it would be a few hours before he could fly. But there was plenty to do in preparation.

By the time they arrived at the Ryder Ranch, Amber had had second, third, even fourth thoughts. Both her father and Hargrove were powerful men. Neither of them took kindly to opposition, and she'd never done anything remotely rebellious in her life.

Hargrove was probably on a plane right now, heading back to Chicago, intending to find her and demand to know what she was *thinking*. And her father was likely out interrogating her friends this morning, determined to find out what had happened and where she'd gone.

Katie would be flabbergasted.

Amber had been questioning her feelings for Hargrove for a couple of months now, but she hadn't shared those fears with Katie. Because, although Katie was a logical and grounded lawyer, she was saddled with an emotional case of hero worship when it came to Hargrove. She thought the sun rose and set on the man. She'd never understand.

Amber had sent her father a final text last night from the airport, assuring him that he didn't need to worry, that she needed some time alone and that she'd be in contact soon. Then she'd turned off her cell phone. She'd seen enough crime dramas to know there were ways to trace the signal. And Hargrove had friends in both high and low places. Where the police couldn't accommodate him, private investigators on the South Side would be happy to wade in.

The sun was emerging from behind the eastern mountains as Amber, Royce and Stephanie crossed the wide porch of the Ryder ranch house. She was dead tired but determined to keep anyone from seeing her mounting worry.

In the rising light of day, she admitted to herself that this had been a colossally stupid plan. Her father and Hargrove weren't going to sit quietly and wait while she worked through her emotions. Plus, she had nothing with her but a pair of high heels, her cocktail dress and a ruby-and-diamond, drop necklace with a set of matching earrings.

And of all the nights to go with a tiny pair of high-cut, sheer panties—sure, they smoothed the line of her dress, but that was their only virtue.

"You heading home?" Royce asked his sister as he tossed a small duffel bag onto the polished hardwood floor, against the wall of a spacious foyer.

"Home," Stephanie echoed, clicking the wide double

doors shut behind her. "I can grab a couple hours' sleep before class starts."

Amber turned to glance quizzically at Stephanie. "Home?" She'd assumed they were already there. The sign on the gate two miles back had clearly stated Ryder Ranch.

"Up to my place." Stephanie pointed. "I've got students arriving this afternoon."

"You don't live here?" Amber kept her voice even, but the thought was unsettling. Sure, Royce was the brother of her father's business associate, but he was still a stranger, and there was safety in numbers.

Stephanie was shaking her head. "They kicked me out years ago."

"When your horses took over the entire yard." Royce loosened his tie and moved out of the foyer. He'd changed out of his tux at the airport in favor of a short-sleeved, white uniform shirt and a pair of navy slacks.

Stephanie made to follow him into a massive, rectangular living room with a two-story, open, timber-beamed ceiling and a bank of glass doors at the far end, flanking a stone fireplace. Amber moved with her, taking in a large, patterned red rug, cream and gold, overstuffed furniture groupings and a huge, round, Western-style chandelier suspended in the center of the room.

"You want me to show Amber a bedroom?" asked Stephanie. She was still wearing her bridesmaid dress.

"She's probably hungry," Royce pointed out, and both looked expectantly at Amber.

"I'm...uh..." The magnitude of her actions suddenly hit Amber. She was standing in a stranger's house, completely dependent on him for food, shelter, even clothes. She was many miles from the nearest town, and every normal support system—her cell phone, credit card and chauffeur—were unavailable to her, since they could be traced.

"Exhausted," Stephanie finished for her, linking an arm with Amber's. "Let's get you upstairs." She gently propelled Amber toward a wide, wooden staircase.

"Good night, then," Royce called from behind them.

"You look shell-shocked," Stephanie whispered in her ear as they mounted the staircase.

"I'm questioning my sanity," Amber admitted as the stairs turned right and walls closed in around them.

Stephanie hit a light switch, revealing a half-octagonal landing, with four doors leading off in separate directions.

"You're not insane," said Stephanie, opening one of the middle doors.

"I just abandoned my fiancé and flew off in the middle of the night with strangers."

"We're not that strange." Stephanie led the way into an airy room that fanned out to a slightly triangular shape.

It had a queen-size, four-poster brass bed, with a blue-and-white-checked comforter that looked decadently soft. Two royal blue armchairs were arranged next to a paned-glass balcony door. White doors led to a walk-in closet and an ensuite bath, while a ceiling fan spun lazily overhead and a cream-colored carpet cushioned Amber's feet.

Stephanie clicked on one of two ceramic bedside lamps. "Or do you think you're insane to leave the fiancé?"

"He's not going to be happy," Amber admitted.

"Does he, like, turn all purple and yell and stuff?" Stephanie looked intrigued and rather excited by the prospect.

Amber couldn't help but smile. "No. He gets all stuffy and logical and superior."

Hargrove would never yell. He'd make Amber feel as though she was a fool, as though her opinions and emotions weren't valid, as though she was behaving like a spoiled child. And maybe she was. But at least she was out of his reach for a little while.

"I hear you." Stephanie opened the double doors of a tall, cherrywood armoire, revealing a set of shelves. "My brothers are like that."

"Royce?" Amber found herself asking. In their admittedly short conversation Royce hadn't seemed at all like Hargrove.

"And Jared," said Stephanie. "They think I'm still ten years old. I'm a full partner in Ryder International, but I have to come to them for every little decision."

"That must be frustrating." Amber sympathized. She had some autonomy with her own credit cards and signing authority on her trust fund. She'd never really thought about independence beyond that.

Well, until now.

"There's this stallion," said Stephanie, selecting something in white cotton from the shelves. "Blanchard's Run, out of Westmont Stables in London. He's perfect for my breeding program. His dam was Ogilvie and his sire Danny Day." She shook her head. "All I need is a million dollars." She handed Amber what turned out to be a cotton nightgown.

"For one horse?" The price sounded pretty high.

"That's mine," said Stephanie, nodding to the gown.

"You should help yourself to anything else in the dresser. There's jeans, shirts, a bunch of stuff that should fit you."

"If it's any consolation," said Amber, putting her hand on Stephanie's arm, "I can't see Hargrove ever letting me spend a million dollars, either."

"And *that's* why you should leave him."

"I'm leaving him—" Amber paused a beat, debating saying the words out loud for the first time "—because I don't love him."

Stephanie's lips formed another silent O. She nodded slowly for a long moment. "Good reason."

Amber agreed.

But she knew her parents would never accept it. And it wasn't because they had some old-fashioned idea about the value of arranged marriages or about love being less important than a person's pedigree. It was because they didn't trust Amber to recognize love one way or the other.

And that was why Amber couldn't go home yet. Nobody would listen to her. They'd all gang up, and she'd find herself railroaded down the aisle.

As usual, it was frighteningly easy for Royce to slip back into the cowboy life. He'd stretched out on his bed for a couple of hours, then dressed in blue jeans, a cotton shirt and his favorite worn cowboy boots. Sasha had quick-fried him a steak, and produced a big stack of hotcakes with maple syrup. After drinking about a gallon of coffee, he'd hunted down the three foremen who reported directly to McQuestin.

He'd learned the vet had recommended moving the Bowler Valley herd because seasonal flies were impacting the calves. A well had broken down at the north camp and the ponds were drying up. And a lumber shipment was stuck at the railhead in Idaho because of a snafu with the letter of credit. But before he'd had a chance to wade in on any of the issues, an SOS had come over his cell phone from Barry Brewster, Ryder International's Vice President of Finance, for a letter from China's Ministry of Trade Development. The original had gone missing in the Chicago office, but they thought Jared might have left a copy at the ranch.

So Royce was wading through the jumble of papers on the messy desk in the front office of the ranch house, looking for a letter from Foreign Investment Director Cheng Li. Without Cheng Li's approval, a deal between Ryder International and Shanxi Electrical would be canceled, costing a fortune, and putting several Ryder construction projects at risk.

Giving up on the desk, and cursing out his older brother for falling in love and getting married at such an inconvenient time, Royce moved to the file cabinet, pulling open the top drawer. His blunt fingers were awkward against the flimsy paper, and the complex numbering system made no sense to him. What the hell was wrong with using the alphabet?

"The outfit seems at odds with the job duties," a female voice ventured from the office doorway.

He turned to see Amber in a pair of snug jeans and a maroon, sleeveless blouse. Her feet were bare, and her blond hair was damp, framing her face in lush waves. There was an amused smile on her fresh, pretty face.

"You think this is funny?" he asked in exasperation.

"Unexpected," she clarified.

"Well, don't just stand there."

"Should I be doing something?"

He directed her to the desktop. "We're looking for a letter from the Chinese Ministry of Trade and Development."

She immediately moved forward.

"Do you know what it looks like?" she asked, picking up the closest pile of papers.

He grunted. "It's on paper."

"Long letter? Short letter? In an envelope? Attached to a report?"

"I don't know. It's from Cheng Li, Foreign Investment Director. I need his phone number."

She moved on to the next pile, while Royce went back to the filing cabinet.

"Have you tried Google?" she asked.

"This isn't the kind of number you find on the Internet."

She continued sorting. "I take it this is important?"

"If I don't get hold of him today, we're going to blow a deal."

"What time is it in China?"

"Sometime Monday morning. Barry says if the approval's not filed in Beijing by the end of business today, we're toast."

"Their time?" Amber asked.

"Their time," Royce confirmed. "What the hell happened to the alphabet?"

She moved closer, brushing against him. "You want me to—"

"No," he snapped, and she quickly halted.

He clamped his jaw and forced himself to take a breath. It wasn't her fault the letter was lost. And it wasn't her fault that his body had a hair-trigger reaction to her touch. "Sorry. Can you keep looking over there? On the desk?"

"Sure." Her features were schooled, and he couldn't tell if she was upset.

"I didn't mean to shout."

"Not a problem." She turned back.

He opened his mouth again, but then decided the conversation could wait. If she was upset, he'd deal with it later. For now, he had three more drawers to search.

"Something to do with Shanxi Electrical?" she asked.

Royce's head jerked up. "You found it?"

She handed him a single sheet of paper.

He scanned his way down to the signature line and found the number for Cheng Li's office. "This is it." He heaved a sigh, resisting the urge to hug her in gratitude.

Then he took in her rosy cheeks, her jewel-blue eyes, her soft hair and smooth skin. The deep colored blouse molded to her feminine curves, while the skintight blue jeans highlighted a killer figure. There was something completely sexy about her bare feet, and he had to fight hard against the urge to hug her.

"Thanks," he offered gruffly, reaching for the phone.

He punched in the international and area codes, then made his way through the rest of the numbers.

After several rings, a voice answered in Chinese at the other end.

"May I speak with Mr. Cheng Li?" he tried.

The voice spoke Chinese again.

"Cheng Li? Is there someone there who speaks English?"

The next words were incomprehensible. He might have heard the name Cheng Li, but he wasn't sure.

"English?" he asked again.

Amber held out her hand and motioned for him to give her the phone.

He gave her a look of incomprehension while the woman on the other end tried once more to communicate with him.

"I'm sorry," he said into the phone, but then it was summarily whisked from his hand.

"Hey!" But before he could protest further, Amber spoke. The words were distinctly non-English.

Royce drew back in astonishment. "No way."

She spoke again. Then she waited. Then she covered the receiver. "Your phone number?" she whispered.

He quickly flipped open his cell to the display, and she rattled something into the phone. Then she finished the call and hung up. "Cheng Li will call you in an hour with an interpreter."

"You speak *Chinese?*" was all Royce could manage.

She gave a self-deprecating eye roll. "I can make myself understood. But for them, it's kind of like talking to a two-year-old."

"You speak Chinese?" he repeated.

"Mandarin, actually." She paused. "I have a knack." When he didn't say anything, she bridged the silence. "My mother taught me Swedish. And I learned Spanish in school." She shrugged. "So, well, considering the potential political impact of the rising Asian economies, I decided Mandarin and Punjabi were the two I should study at college. I'm really not that good at either of them."

He peered at her. "You're like a politician's dream wife, aren't you?"

Her lips pursed for a moment, and discomfort flickered in her eyes. "Are you saying I have no life?"

"I'm saying he's going to come after you." Royce put a warning in his tone. "I sure as hell wouldn't let you get away."

She blinked, and humor came back into her blue eyes. "I doubt I'd make it very far from here. After all, there is only one road out of the ranch."

Royce wasn't in the mood to joke. "He *is* going to come after you, isn't he?"

She sobered. "I don't think he'll find me."

"And if he does?"

She didn't answer.

"What's the guy got on you?"

From what Royce could see, Amber was an intelligent, capable woman. There was no reason in the world for her to let herself get saddled with a man she didn't want.

"Same thing Jared has on you," she answered softly. "Duty, obligation, guilt."

"Jared needs me for a month," said Royce, not buying into the parallel. "What's-his-name—"

"Hargrove."

"Hargrove wants you forever." Royce felt a sudden spurt of anger. "And where the hell are your parents in all this? Have you told them?"

"They think he's perfect for me."

"He's not."

Amber smiled. "You've never even met him."

"I don't have to. You're here. He's there." Royce ran

his brain through the circumstances one more time. "Your cell's turned off, right?"

She nodded.

"Don't use your credit cards."

"I didn't bring them."

"Good."

"Not really." She hesitated. "Royce, I have no money whatsoever."

"You don't need money."

"And I have no clothes, not even underwear."

Okay, that gave him an unwanted visual. "We have everything you need right here."

"I can't live off your charity."

"You're our guest."

"I forced you to bring me here."

Royce set the letter back down on the desktop and tucked his phone back into his shirt pocket. "Ask anybody, Amber. I don't do anything I don't want to do." He let his gaze shade the meaning of the words. He'd brought her home with him because she was a beautiful and interesting woman. It was absolutely no hardship having her around.

"I need to earn my keep."

Royce resisted the temptation to make a joke about paying her way by sleeping with him. It was in poor taste, and the last thing he wanted to do was insult her. Besides, the two were completely unrelated.

He hoped she was attracted to him. What red-blooded man wouldn't? And last night he had been fairly certain she was attracted to him. But whatever was between them would take its own course.

Her gaze strayed to the messy desk. "I could…"

He followed the look.

"…maybe straighten things up a little? I've taken business management courses, some accounting—"

"No argument from me." Royce held up his palms in surrender. "McQuestin's niece, Maddy, usually helps out in the office, but she's gone back to Texas with him while he recovers." He spread his arms in welcome. "Make yourself at home."

Three

Several hours later, eyes grainy from reading ranch paperwork, Amber wandered out of the office. The office door opened into a short hallway that connected to the front foyer and then to the rest of the ranch house. It had grown dark while she worked, and soft lamplight greeted her in the empty living room. The August night was cool, with pale curtains billowing in the side windows, while screen doors separated the room from the veranda beyond.

Muted noise came from the direction of the kitchen, and she caught a movement on the veranda. Moving closer, she realized it was a plump puff ball of a black-and-white puppy. Amber smiled in reaction as another pup appeared, and then a third and a fourth.

They hadn't seen her yet, and the screen door kept them locked outside. Just as well. They were cute, but

Amber was a little intimidated by animals. She'd never had a pet before. Her mother didn't like the noise, the mess or the smell.

Truth was, she dropped out of dressage riding lessons because one of the horses had bit her on the shoulder. She hadn't told the grooms, or her parents, or anybody else about the incident. She was embarrassed, convinced that she'd done something to annoy the horse but not sure of what it might have been. When a creature couldn't talk or communicate, how did you know what they wanted or needed?

The pups disappeared from view, and she moved closer to the door, peeking at an angle to see them milling in a small herd around Royce's feet while he sat in a deep, wooden Adirondack chair, reading some kind of report under the half-dozen outdoor lamps that shone around the veranda.

Then the pups spotted her and made a roly-poly beeline for the door, sixteen paws thumping awkwardly on the wooden slats of the deck. She took an automatic step back as they piled up against the screen.

Royce glanced up from the papers. "Hey, Amber." Then his attention went to the puppies. He gave a low whistle, and they scampered back to him.

"It's safe to come out now," he said with a warm smile.

"I'm not…" She eased the door open. "I'm not scared to come out."

Royce laughed. "Didn't think you were. Shut the screen behind you, though, or these guys will be in the kitchen in a heartbeat."

She closed the screen door behind her. "Your puppies?"

He reached down to scratch between the ears of the full-grown border collie sprawled between the chair and the railing. "They belong to Molly. Care to take one home when you leave?"

"My mother won't have pets in the house." The puppies rushed back to Amber again.

Royce gestured for her to take the chair across from his. "Is she allergic?"

"Not exactly." Warm, fuzzy bodies pressed against her leg; cool, wet noses investigated her bare feet and she felt a mushy tongue across the top of her toes. She struggled not to cringe at the slimy sensation. "She doesn't want any accidents on the Persian rug."

"The price you pay," said Royce.

Amber settled into the chair. One of the pups put its paws on her knee, lifting up to sniff along her jeans.

"Most people pet them." Royce's tone was wry.

"I'm a little..." She gingerly scratched the puppy between its floppy, little ears. Its fur was soft, skin warm, and its dark eyes were adorable.

"It's okay," he said. "Not everybody likes animals."

"I don't dislike them."

"I can tell."

"They make me a little nervous, okay?"

"They're puppies, not mountain lions."

"They—" Another warm tongue swiped across her bare toes, and she jerked her feet under the chair. "Tickle," she finished.

"Princess," he mocked her.

"I was once bitten by a horse," she defended. Her interactions with animals hadn't been particularly positive so far.

"I was once gored by a bull," he countered with a challenging look.

"Is this going to be a contest?"

"Kicked in the head." He leaned forward and parted his short, dark hair.

She couldn't see a scar, but she trusted it was there.

"By a bronc," he finished. "In a local rodeo at fourteen."

Amber lifted her elbow to show a small scar. "Fell off a top bunk. At camp. I was *thirteen*."

"Did you break it?"

"Sprained."

"What kind of camp?"

"Violin."

His grin went wide. "Oh, my. Such a dangerous life. Did you ever break a nail? Get a bad wax job?"

"Hey, buddy." She jabbed her finger in the direction of his chest. "*After* your first wax job, we can talk."

Devilment glowed in his deep blue eyes. "You can wax anything I've got," he drawled. "Any ol' time you want."

Her stomach contracted, and a wave of unexpected heat prickled her skin. How had the conversation taken that particular turn? She sat up straight and folded her hands primly in her lap. "That's not what I meant."

He paused, gaze going soft. "That's too bad."

The puppies had grown bored with her feet, and one by one, they'd wandered back to Royce. They were now curled in a sleeping heap around his chair. The dog, Molly, yawned while insects made dancing shadows in the veranda lights.

"You hungry?" asked Royce.

Amber nodded. She was starving, and she was more than happy to let their discussion die.

He flipped the report closed, and she was reminded of their earlier office work.

"Did you talk to Cheng Li?"

"I did," said Royce. "He promised to fax the paperwork to the Ryder financial office."

"In Chicago."

"Yes." He rose cautiously to his feet, stepping around the sleeping puppies. "Disaster averted. Sasha'll have soup on the stove."

"Soup sounds great." It was nearly nine, and Amber hadn't eaten anything since their light snack on the plane around 5:00 a.m. Any kind of food sounded terrific to her right now.

They left the border collies asleep on the deck and filed through the living room, down a hallway to the kitchen on the south side of the house.

"Have you talked to your parents?" asked Royce as he set a pair of blue-glazed, stoneware bowls out on the breakfast bar.

The counters were granite, the cabinets dark cherry. There were stainless steel appliances with cheery, yellow walls and ceiling reflecting off the polished beams and natural wood floor. A trio of spotlights was suspended above the bar, complementing the glow of the pot lights around the perimeter of the ceiling.

"I texted them both before I got on the plane."

"Nothing since then?" He set a basket of grainy buns on the breakfast bar, and she slipped onto one of the high, padded, hunter-green leather chairs.

She shook her head. "I don't know how this GPS and triangulating-the-cell-towers thing works."

Royce's brows went up, and he paused in his work.

"Crime dramas," she explained. "I don't know how much of all that is fiction. My dad, and Hargrove for sure, will pull out all the stops."

Royce held out his hand. "Let me see your phone."

She pulled back on the stool and dug the little phone out of the pocket of her blue jeans.

He slid it open and pressed the on button.

"Are you sure—"

"I won't leave it on long." He peered at the tiny screen. "Nope. No GPS function." He shut it off and tossed it back to her. "Though they could, theoretically, triangulate while you're talking, but you're probably safe to text."

"Really?" That was good news. She'd like to send another message to her mother. And Katie deserved an explanation.

He set out two small plates and spoons while she tucked the phone back into her pocket. She'd have to think about how to phrase her explanation.

Royce ladled the steaming soup into the bowls and set them back on the bar, taking the stool at the end.

"Thanks," she breathed, inhaling the delectable aroma.

Royce lifted his spoon. "So, how long have you known?"

She followed suit, dipping into the rich broth. "Known what?"

"That you didn't love him?"

Royce knew his question was blunt to the point of rudeness, but if he was going to make a play for Amber, he needed to know the lay of the land. He knew he'd be a temporary, rebound fling, which was not even remotely a problem for him. In fact, he'd gone into the situation *planning* to be her temporary, rebound fling. She wasn't going to stay the whole month. She probably wouldn't even last a week. But he was up for it, however long it lasted.

Last night, he'd known Amber was beautiful. Today, he'd learned she was positively fascinating. She was intelligent, poised and personable, and she could actually speak Chinese. Her reaction to the puppies was cute and endearing. While her fiancé's and family's ability to intimidate her made him curious.

Why would such an accomplished woman give a rat's hind end what anybody thought of her decisions?

She stirred her spoon thoughtfully through the bowl of soup. "It's not so much…" she began.

He waited.

She looked up. "It's not that I knew I didn't love him. It's more that I didn't know that I did. You know?"

Royce hadn't the slightest idea what she meant, and he shook his head.

"It seems to me," she said, cocking her head sideways, teeth raking momentarily over her full bottom lip, "if you're going to say 'till death do us part' you'd better be damn sure."

Royce couldn't disagree with that. His parents obviously hadn't been damn sure. At least his mother wasn't. His father, on the other hand, had to have been devastated by her betrayal.

Amber was right to break it off. She had absolutely no business marrying a man she didn't love unreservedly.

"You'd better be damn sure," Royce echoed, fighting a feeling of annoyance with her for even considering marrying a man she didn't love. This Hargrove person might be a jerk. So far, he sounded like a jerk. But no man deserved a disloyal wife.

Amber nodded as she swallowed a spoonful of the soup. "Melissa looked sure."

"Melissa *was* sure."

Amber blinked at the edge to Royce's tone. "What?"

"Nothing." He tore a bun in half.

"You annoyed?"

He shook his head.

"Melissa and Jared seem really good together."

"You do know it's kinder to break it off up front with a guy." Royce set down his spoon.

"I—"

"Because, if you don't, the next thing you know, you'll have two or three kids, the PTA and carpool duty. You'll get bored. You'll start looking around. And you'll end up at the No-Tell Motel on Route 55, in bed with some young drifter. And Hargrove, whoever-he-is, will be going for his gun."

"Whoa." Amber's eyes were wide in the stark kitchen light. "You just did my whole life in thirty seconds."

"I didn't necessarily mean you."

"What? Are we talking about Melissa?"

"No." Royce gave himself a mental shake. "We are absolutely not talking about Melissa."

"Then who—"

"Nobody. Forget it." He drew a breath. So much for making a play for her. It wouldn't be tonight. That was for sure. "I just don't understand why you're feeling guilty," he continued. "You are absolutely doing the right thing."

"I believe that," she agreed.

He held her gaze with a frank stare. "And anybody who tries to talk you out of it is shortsighted and just plain stupid."

"You know you're talking about my father."

"I know."

"He's Chairman of the City Accountants Association, and he owns a multimillion-dollar financial consortium."

"Pure blind luck, obviously."

A small smile crept out, though she clearly fought against it. "The No-Tell Motel?"

"Metaphorically speaking. I'm sure you'd pick the Ritz."

"I've never been unfaithful."

Royce knew he should apologize.

"I've dated Hargrove since I was eighteen, and even though he's not the greatest—" She snapped her mouth shut, and a flush rose in her cheeks as she reached for one of the homemade buns.

Okay, this was interesting. "Not the greatest what?"

"Nothing."

"You're blushing."

"No, I'm not." She tore into the bun.

Royce grinned. "Were you going to say *lover?*"

"No." But everything in her body language told him she was lying.

He gazed at her profile for a long minute.

Eighteen. She was eighteen when she took up with Hargrove. Royce could be wrong, but he didn't think he was. Amber hadn't had any other lovers. She was dissatisfied with Hargrove, but she had no comparison.

Interesting. He chewed a hunk of his own bun.

A woman deserved at least one comparison.

"What did you find?" Royce's voice from the office doorway interrupted Amber's long day of office work.

The sun was descending toward the rugged mountains, while neat piles of bills and correspondence had slowly grown out of the chaos on the desktop in front of her.

Now she stretched her arm out to place a letter on the farthest pile. It was another advertisement for horse tack. She was fairly sure the junk mail could be tossed out, but she wasn't about to make that decision on her own.

"You've got some overdue bills," she answered Royce, twisting her head to see him lounging in the doorway, one broad shoulder propped against the doorjamb, his hair mussed and sweaty across his forehead and a streak of dirt marring his roughened chin. She met his deep blue gaze, and a surge of longing clenched her chest.

"Pay them," he suggested in a sexy rumble, crossing his arms over his chest.

"You going to hand over your platinum card?"

His lips parted in a grin. "Sure."

"Then you better have a high limit. Some of them are six figures." Feed, lumber, vet bills. The list went on and on.

He eased away from the door frame and ambled toward her. "There must be a checkbook around here somewhere."

"I didn't see one." Not that she'd combed through the desk drawers. There was plenty to do sorting through what was piled on top. "How long did you say McQuestin had been off?"

"Three weeks. Why?"

"Some of these bills are two months old. That's hell on your credit rating, you know."

He moved closer, and she forced herself to drag her gaze from his rangy body.

To distract herself, she lifted the closest unopened envelope and sliced through the seam with the ivory-handled opener, extracting another folded invoice. The distraction didn't help. Her nostrils picked up his fresh, outdoorsy scent, and his arm brushed her shoulder, sending an electric current over her skin as he slid open a top desk drawer.

Lifting several items out of the way, he quickly produced a narrow, leather-bound booklet and tossed it on the desk. "Here you go. Start protecting my credit rating."

"Like the bank would honor my signature." She knew she should shift away, but something magnetic kept her sitting right where she was, next to his narrow hip and strong thigh. She didn't even care that his jeans were dusty.

Not that it would matter if anything rubbed off. She was dressed in a plain, khaki T-shirt and a pair of faded jeans she'd borrowed from Stephanie's cache in the upstairs bedroom. She could press herself against Royce from head to toe, and simply clean up later with soap and water.

The idea was far too appealing. She felt heat flare in the pit of her stomach as an image bloomed in her mind.

"I'll sign a bunch for you." His voice interrupted her burgeoning fantasy as he flipped open the checkbook.

She blinked herself back to reality. "I assume you're joking."

"Why would I be joking?" He leaned over, hunting through the drawer again, bringing himself into even closer contact with her.

She shifted imperceptibly in his direction, and his cotton-clad arm brushed her bare one. She sucked in a tight breath.

He retrieved a pen.

She suddenly realized he was serious, and placed her hand over the top check. "You can't do that."

He turned, pen poised, bringing their faces into close proximity. "Why not?"

"Because I could write myself a check, a *very big* check, and then cash it."

He rolled his eyes

"Don't give me that 'shucks ma'am' expression—"

"'Shucks, ma'am'?"

"You didn't just wander in off the back forty. You know I could drain your account."

"Would you?"

"I *could,*" she stressed. Theoretically, of course.

He twirled the pen over two fingers until it settled into his palm. "And then what?"

"And then I disappear. Tahiti, Grand Cayman."

"I'd find you."

"So what?" She shrugged. "What could you do? The money would already be in a Swiss bank account."

He braced one hand against the desk and moved the other to the back of her chair, bending slightly over. "Then I'd ask you, politely, for the number."

She was blocked by the V of his arms. It was

unnerving, but also exciting. He emanated strength, power and raw virility.

"And if I refuse to tell you?" she challenged, voice growing breathy.

"I'd stop being polite."

"What? You'd threaten to break my legs?"

He smiled and leaned closer. Self-preservation told her to shrink away, but the chair back kept her in place. His sweet breath puffed against her skin. "Violence? I don't think so. But there are other ways to be persuasive."

She struggled for a tone of disbelief. "What? You kiss me and I swoon?"

His grin widened. "Maybe. Let's try it."

And before she could react, he'd swooped in toward her. She gasped as his smooth lips settled on hers. They were warm and firm, and incredibly hot, as the contact instantly escalated to a serious kiss.

It took her only seconds to realize how much she'd longed for his taste. His scent filled her, and his hands settled on her sides, surrounding her rib cage as he deepened the kiss. Her head tipped back, and her mouth responded to his pressure by opening, allowing him access, drinking in the sensation of his intimate touch.

She clutched his upper arms, steadying herself against his hard, taut muscles. He flexed under her touch, and she imagined she could feel the blood coursing through his body. She could definitely feel the blood coursing through her own. It heated her core, flushed her skin and made her tingle from the roots of her hair to the tips of her toes.

His hands convulsed against her body, thumbs tightening beneath her breasts. Her nipples hardened almost painfully as arousal thumped its way to the apex of her thighs. She gave him her tongue, answering his own erotic invitation. A river of sound roared in her ears as he drew her to her feet, engulfing her, pressing her against his hard body.

His touch was unique, yet achingly familiar, as if she'd been waiting for this moment her entire life. Her palms slid across his shoulders, around his neck, stroking the slick sweat of his hairline as their kiss pulsed endlessly between them.

His hands slipped to her buttocks, pulling her against the cradle of his thighs, demonstrating the depth of his arousal and shocking her back to her senses.

She jerked away, hands pressing against his chest, putting a barrier between them. He leaned in, trying to capture her mouth.

"I can't," she gasped.

He froze.

"I'm…uh…" She wasn't exactly sorry. That had definitely been the best kiss of her life. But she couldn't take things any further. They barely knew each other. She'd only just left Hargrove. And she hadn't come to Montana for casual sex.

"Something wrong?" he asked.

She tried to take a step back, but the damn chair still blocked her way. "This is too fast," she explained, struggling to bring both her breathing and her pulse rate back under control.

He heaved an exasperated sigh. "It was a kiss, Amber."

But they both knew it was more than a kiss. Then, to her mortification, her gaze reflexively flicked below his waistline.

He gave a knowing chuckle, and she wished the floor would swallow her whole.

"Are you blushing?" he asked.

"No." But she couldn't look him in the eyes.

"You seemed a whole lot more sophisticated when we met in the lounge," he ventured.

She couldn't interpret his flat tone, so she braved a glance at his expression. Was he annoyed?

He looked annoyed.

She hadn't intended to lead him on. Nor had she meant for the kiss to spiral out of control.

Surely he could understand that.

Or was he always so quick to leap to expectations?

Then, an unsettling thought hit her. What if Royce hadn't leaped to expectations in the past two minutes? What if his expectations had been there since their meeting in the lounge?

Had she been hopelessly naive? Did he consider her a one- or two-night stand?

"Is *that* why you brought me here?" she asked, watching closely, giving him the chance to deny it.

"Depends," he said, cocking his head and giving her a considering look. "On what you mean by *that*."

"Because you thought I'd sleep with you?"

"It had crossed my mind," he admitted.

Her embarrassment turned to anger. "Seriously?"

He sighed. "Amber—"

"You are the most egotistical, opportunistic—"

"Hey, you were the one who was dressed to kill and insisted on 'taking a ride in my jet plane.'"

"That *wasn't* a euphemism for sex."

"Really?" He looked genuinely surprised. "It usually is."

Amber compressed her lips. How had she been so naive? How could she have been so incredibly foolish? Royce wasn't some knight in shining armor. He was a charming, wealthy, well-groomed pickup artist.

Her distaste was replaced again by embarrassment. She'd proposed paying her way here by doing office work. He'd had a completely different line of work in mind.

She pushed the wheeled chair aside and moved to go around him. "I think I'd better leave."

She'd have to call her parents to rescue her, head back to Chicago with her tail between her legs, maybe even reconsider her relationship with Hargrove, since, as the three of them so often told her, she was naive in the ways of the real world.

At least with Hargrove, she knew where she stood.

"Why?" Royce asked, putting a hand on her arm to stop her.

She glanced at his hand, and he immediately let go.

"There's obviously been a misunderstanding." She'd hang out in the upstairs bedroom until a car could come for her. Then she'd head back to the airport, home to her parents' mansion and back to her real life.

This had been a crazy idea from beginning to end.

"Clearly," said Royce, his jaw tight.

She moved toward the door.

Royce's voice followed her. "Running back to Mommy and Daddy?"

Her spine straightened. "None of your business."

"What's changed?" he challenged.

She reached for the doorknob.

"What's changed, Amber?" he repeated.

She paused. Then she turned to confront him. No

point in beating around the bush. "I thought I was a houseguest. You thought I was a call girl."

A grin quirked one corner of his mouth, and her anger flared anew.

"Are you always this melodramatic?" he asked.

"Shut up."

He shook his head and took a couple of steps toward her. "I meant what's changed on your home front?"

"Nothing," she admitted, except it had occurred to her that her parents might be right. She had been protected from the real world for most of her life. Maybe she wasn't in a position to judge human nature. They'd always insisted Hargrove was the perfect man for her, and they could very well be right.

"So, why go back?" Royce pressed.

"Where else would I go?" She could sneak off to some other part of the country, but her father would track her down as soon as she accessed her bank account. Besides, the longer she stayed away, the more awkward the reunion.

Royce took another step forward. "You don't have to leave."

She scoffed out a dry laugh.

"I never thought you were a call girl."

"You thought I was a barroom pickup."

"True enough," he agreed. "But only because it's happened so many times before."

"You're *bragging?*"

"Just stating the facts."

She scoffed at his colossal ego.

"You're welcome to stay as a houseguest." He sounded sincere.

"Are you kidding?" She couldn't imagine anything

more uncomfortable. He'd been planning to sleep with her. And for a few seconds there, well, sleeping with Royce hadn't seemed like such a bad idea. And he must have known it. She was sure he'd known it.

Their gazes held.

"I can control myself if you can," he told her.

"There's nothing for me to control," she insisted.

He let her lie slide. "Good. Then it's settled."

"Nothing is—"

He nodded toward the desk. "You organize my office and pay my bills, and I'll keep my hands to myself." He paused. "Unless, of course, you change your mind about my hands."

"I'm not going to—"

He held up a hand to silence her. "Let's not make any promises we're going to regret."

She let her glare do the talking, but a little voice inside her acknowledged he was right. She didn't plan to change her mind. But for a few minutes there, it had been easy enough to imagine his hands all over her body.

Four

Royce felt the burn in his shoulder muscles as he hefted another stack of two-by-fours from the flatbed to a waiting pickup truck. The two ranch hands assigned to the task had greeted him with obvious curiosity when he joined the work crew. Hauling lumber in the dark, with the smell of rain in the air, was hardly a choice assignment.

But Royce needed to work the frustration out of his system somehow. How had he so completely misjudged Amber's signals? He could have sworn she was as into him as he was her.

He slid the heavy stack across the dropped tailgate and shifted it to the front of the box, admitting that he'd deluded himself the past few months in the hotel fitness rooms. High-tech exercise equipment was no match for the sweat of real work.

"Something wrong?" came Stephanie's voice as she appeared beside him in the pool of the yard light. She tugged a pair of leather work gloves from the back pocket of her jeans. "You looked ticked off."

"Nothing's wrong," Royce denied, turning on the dirt track to retrace his steps to the flatbed, passing the two hands who were on the opposite cycle. "Where'd you come from?"

Stephanie slipped her hands into the gloves, lifting two boards to Royce's five, balancing them on her right shoulder. "I drove down to join you for dinner. I wanted to see how Amber was doing."

"She's fine.

"She inside?"

He shrugged. "I assume so."

"You have a fight?"

"No. We didn't have a fight." An argument, maybe. In fact, it was more of a misunderstanding. And it was none of his sister's damn business.

"Something wrong with Bar—"

"No!" Royce practically shouted. Wait a minute. His sister might have changed topics. He forced himself to calm down. "What?"

"With Barry Brewster," she enunciated. "Our VP of finance? I talked to him earlier, and he sounded weird."

Royce slid his load into the pickup then lifted the boards from Stephanie's shoulder and placed them in the box. "Weird how?"

It was Stephanie's turn to shrug. "He yelled at me."

Royce's brow went up. "He *what?*"

They stepped out of the way of the two hands each carrying a load of lumber.

Stephanie lowered her voice. "With Jared gone. Well, Blanchard's Sun, an offspring of Blanchard's Run, took silver at Dannyville Downs, and—"

"*S-o-n* son?" Royce asked.

"*S-u-n*. It's a mare."

"You don't think that will get confusing?"

Stephanie frowned at him. "I didn't name her."

"Still—"

"Try to stay on topic."

"Right."

The temperature dropped a few degrees. The wind picked up, and ozone snapped in the air. Royce went back to work, knowing the rain wasn't far off.

Stephanie followed. "Blanchard's Run is proving to be an incredible sire. With every week that passes, his price will go up. So I called Barry to talk about moving some funds to the stable account."

"Did you really expect him to hand over a million?"

"Sure." She paused, sucking in a breath as she hefted some more lumber. "Maybe. Okay, it was a long shot. But that's not my point."

"What is your point?"

The first, fat raindrops clanked on the truck's roof, and one of the hands retrieved an orange tarp from the shed. Royce increased his pace to settle the last of the lumber on the pickup, then accepted the large square of plastic.

"You two get the flatbed," he instructed, motioning for Stephanie to move to the other side of the pickup box.

"My point," Stephanie called over the clatter from

the tarp under the increasing rain, "is Barry's reaction. He went off on me about cash flow and interest rates."

"Over a million dollars?" Royce threaded a nylon rope through the corner grommet of the tarp and looped it around the tie-down on the running board. It was a lot to pay for a horse, sure. But there weren't enough zeros in the equation to raise Barry's blood pressure.

"I felt like a ten-year-old asking for her allowance."

"That's because you behave like a ten-year-old." Royce tossed the rope over the load to his sister.

"It's a great deal," she insisted as lightning cracked the sky above them. "If we don't move now, it'll be gone forever."

"Isn't that what you said about Nare-Do-Elle?"

"That was three years ago."

"He cost us a bundle."

"This is a completely different circumstance. I'm right this time." She tossed the rope back. "You don't think I've learned anything in three years?"

Royce cinched down the tarp. He wasn't touching that question with a ten-foot cattle prod. "What exactly do you want me to do?" he asked instead.

"Talk to Barry."

"And say what?"

"Tell him to give me the money."

Royce grinned.

"I'm serious." The rain had soaked into her curly auburn hair, dampening her cheeks, streaking down her freckled nose.

"You're always serious. You always need money. And half the time you're wrong."

She waggled her leather gloved finger at him. "And half the time I'm *right*."

"So I'll get you half a million."

"And you'll lose out on generations of champion jumpers."

Royce walked the rope around the back of the pickup, tying it off on the fourth corner. "Sorry, Steph."

Her hands went to her hips. "I own a third of this company."

"And I have Jared's power of attorney."

"You two have *always* ganged up on me."

"Now you're sounding like a child."

"I'm—"

"I'm not giving a million dollars to a child."

Her chin tipped up. "You weren't giving it to me anyway."

"True," Royce admitted. He couldn't resist chucking her under that defiant chin. "You've got a perfectly adequate operating budget. Live within your means."

"This is an extraordinary opportunity. I can't begin to tell you—"

"There'll be another one tomorrow. Or next week. Or next month." He'd known his sister far too long to fall for her impassioned plea.

"That's not fair."

"Life never is."

Thunder clapped above them, and the heavens opened up, the deluge soaking everything in sight. The ranch hands ran for the cook shed, and Royce grabbed Stephanie's hand, tugging her over the muddy ground toward the lights of the house.

Amber stood in the vast Ryder living room, rain pounding on the ceiling and clattering against the windows in the waning daylight as she stared at the cell phone in her hand. Royce had been a gentleman about it, but that didn't change the fact that she'd put herself in a predicament and behaved less responsibly than she'd admitted to herself.

She really needed to let someone know where she was staying. She also needed to make sure her parents weren't worrying about her. Her father tended to blow things out of proportion, and there was a real chance he was freeing up cash, waiting for a ransom note.

She pressed the on button with her thumb, deciding she'd keep it short and simple.

"Calling in the cavalry?" came Royce's dry voice.

Amber glanced up to see him and Stephanie in the archway leading from the front foyer.

"Did you hear the thunder?" Stephanie grinned as she stepped forward, stripping off a pair of leather gloves and running spread fingers through her unruly, wet hair.

Amber nodded. The storm had heightened her sense of isolation and disquiet.

"I love storms," Stephanie continued, dropping the gloves on an end table. "As long as I'm inside." She frowned, glancing down at her wet clothes. "I'm going upstairs to find something dry. Is that lasagna I smell?" Her pert nose wrinkled.

Amber inhaled the aromas wafting from the kitchen. "I think so."

"My fav." Stephanie smiled. "See you in a few." She skipped up the stairs.

As he stood there in the doorway, the planes and angles of Royce's face were emphasized by the yellow lamplight reflecting off the wood grain walls.

An hour ago, she'd come to the conclusion that she couldn't really blame him for thinking she was attracted to him. She imagined most women who requested a ride in his plane were coming on to him. Not that she blamed them. His shoulders were broad in his work clothes. His dark, wet hair glimmered, and those deep blue eyes seemed to stare right down into a woman's soul.

"Did you decide to leave after all?" he asked, his deep voice reverberating through her body, igniting a fresh wave of desire.

She shook her head. "I'm just reassuring my parents."

Royce moved into the room with an easy, rolling gait. He struck her as different than the man in the hotel lobby lounge. In just a couple of days, the wilds of Montana had somehow seeped into him.

"Not worried they'll track you down?" His steps slowed as he stopped in front of her, slightly closer than socially acceptable, just a few inches into her personal space, and she felt her heartbeat deepen.

"I'm worried they might be raising the ransom."

Royce quirked a brow. "Seriously?"

"I've never done anything like this before."

"No kidding."

"Royce." She wasn't sure what she was going to say to him, or how she should say it.

But before she could formulate the words, his voice and expression went soft. "I'm sorry."

She shook her head. "No. I'm the one who's sorry. I gave you the wrong impression. It wasn't on purpose, but I realize now that—"

"It was wishful thinking on my part."

"You flat out told me you were hitting on me."

"I was."

She fought a reflexive smile. "And I'm honored." She found herself joking.

"I don't want you to be honored." His expression said the rest.

"I know exactly what you want."

He eased almost imperceptibly closer. "Yes, you do."

They both went silent, sobering. Thunder rumbled overhead, and the moisture-laden air hung heavily in the room.

Stephanie's light footsteps sounded on the landing above.

"You should make that call," said Royce, stepping back.

Amber nodded, struggling to get her hormones under control. She'd never been pursued by such a rawly masculine man. Come to think of it, she'd never been pursued by any man.

Oh, she received her fair share of flirtatious overtures on a girls' night at the clubs, but a flash of her engagement ring easily shut the guys down. Plus, usually she was out with Hargrove. And they generally attended functions where he was known. Nobody was about to hit on Hargrove Alston's fiancée.

While Stephanie skipped down the stairs, Amber pressed the speed-dial button for her mother. It rang only once.

"Sweetheart!" came her mother's voice. "What happened? Are you okay? Are you having a break-down?"

Amber turned away from Royce, crossing the few steps to an alcove where she'd have a little privacy.

"I'm fine," she answered, ignoring the part about a breakdown.

"Your father is beside himself."

Royce's and Stephanie's footfalls faded toward the kitchen.

"And Hargrove," her mother continued. "He came home a day early. Then he nearly missed the Chamber dinner tonight worrying about you. He was the keynote, you know."

"He *nearly* missed it?" asked Amber, finding a hard tone in her voice. Hargrove hadn't, in fact, missed his big speech while his beloved fiancée was missing, perhaps kidnapped, maybe dead.

As soon as the thoughts formed in her mind, she realized she was being unfair. She'd sent a text saying she was fine, and she had expected them to believe her. She wanted Hargrove to carry on with his life.

"The Governor was there," her mother defended.

"I'm glad he went to the dinner," said Amber.

"Where are you? I'll send a car."

"I'm not coming back yet."

"Why not?"

"Didn't Dad tell you?"

"That nonsense about not marrying Hargrove? That's crazy talk, darling. He wowed them last night."

"He didn't wow me." As soon as the words slipped out, Amber clamped her lips shut.

"You weren't there." Her mother either missed or ignored the double entendre.

"I wanted to let you know I'm fine." Amber got back on point.

"Where are you?"

"It doesn't matter."

"Of *course* it matters. We need to get you—"

"Not yet."

"Amber—"

"I'll call again soon." Amber didn't know how long it took to trace a cell phone call, but she suspected she should hurry and hang up.

"What do you expect me to tell your father?"

"Tell him not to worry. I love you both, and I'll call again. Bye, Mom." She quickly disconnected.

A slightly plump, fiftyish woman, who Amber had earlier learned was Sasha, was pulling a large pan of lasagna from the stainless steel oven when Amber entered the kitchen. Stephanie was tossing a salad in a carved wooden bowl on the breakfast bar, while Royce transferred warm rolls into a linen-napkin-lined basket.

For the second time, she was struck by his domesticity. The men she knew didn't help out in the kitchen. Come to think of it, the women she knew didn't, either. And though Amber herself had taken French cooking lessons at her private school, the lessons had centered more on choosing a caterer than hands-on cooking.

"There's a wine cooler around the corner." Stephanie was looking to Amber as she indicated the direction with a toss of her auburn head. "Italian wines are on the third tier, left-hand side."

Royce didn't turn as Amber made her way to a small alcove between the kitchen and the back entryway. The cooler was set in a stone wall, reds in one glass-fronted compartment, whites in the other.

"See if there's a Redigaffi." Royce's voice was so close behind her that it gave her a start.

She took a bracing breath and opened the glass door, turning a couple of bottles on the third shelf so that she could see their labels.

"How'd the call go?" he asked.

"Fine."

There was a silence.

"That's it?" he asked. "Fine?"

"I talked to my mother. She wants me to come home." Amber found the right bottle of wine and slid it out of the holder, straightening and turning to discover Royce was closer than she'd expected. She pushed the glass door closed behind her.

"And?" he asked.

"And what?" She reflexively clutched the bottle.

"Are you going home?"

Though they'd agreed she'd merely be a houseguest, the question seemed loaded with meaning as his eyes thoroughly searched her expression.

"Not yet," she answered.

"Good."

She felt the need to clarify. "It doesn't mean—"

"I meant it's good because you don't love Hargrove, so it would be stupid to go back."

She gave him a short nod.

"Not that the other's gone away," he clarified.

Amber didn't know how to respond to that.

His gaze moved to the bottle. "Did you find one?"

She raised it, and he lifted it from her hands.

"Perfect," he said.

"Move your butts," called Stephanie from the kitchen, and Amber suddenly realized that her world had contracted to the tiny alcove, Royce and her wayward longings.

She gave herself a mental shake, while he took a step back and gestured for her to lead the way into the kitchen.

Stephanie was setting wineglasses at three places at the breakfast bar, while Sasha had disappeared. The Ryder family was a curious mix of informality and luxury. The glasses were fine, blown crystal. The wine was from an exquisite vineyard that Amber recognized. But they were hopping up on high chairs at the breakfast bar to a plain, white casserole pan of simple, beef lasagna.

"Did you talk to your mom?" asked Stephanie as she took the end seat.

Amber took the one around the corner, and Royce settled next to her. He was both too close and too far away. She could almost detect the heat of his body, felt the change in air currents while he moved, and she was overcome with a potent desire to touch him. Of course, touching him was out of the question.

"I talked to her," she told Stephanie.

"What did she say?"

"She wants me to come home and, well, reconcile with Hargrove, of course."

"And?" Stephanie pressed. "What did you tell her?"

"That I wasn't ready." Amber found herself deliberately not looking in Royce's direction as she spoke.

"Good for you," said Stephanie with a vigorous nod. "We girls, we have to stick to our guns. There are too many people in our lives trying to interfere with our decisions." She cast a pointed gaze at her brother.

"Give it a rest," Royce growled at his sister, twisting the corkscrew into the top of the wine. "You're not getting a million dollars."

"You're such a hard-ass."

"And you're a spoiled brat."

"You *are* spending an awful lot for vet supplies and lumber," Amber put in. "Those are the bills I found stacked up on the office desk."

Stephanie blinked at her. "Oh."

Royce popped the cork and reached for Amber's wineglass. "Amber has some questions about the accounts. Who does McQuestin deal with at head office?"

"I think he talks to Norma Braddock sometimes."

Royce handed the wine bottle to his sister then whisked his cell phone from his pocket. "I'll go straight to Barry."

"I'd watch out for him," Stephanie advised, forehead wrinkling.

Royce rolled his eyes at the warning.

Amber decided to stay quiet.

"Barry?" said Royce, while Stephanie handed the salad bowl to Amber.

Amber served herself some of the freshest-looking lettuce and tomatoes she'd ever seen.

"Royce, here."

Then she leaned toward Stephanie and whispered, "From your garden?"

Stephanie nodded, whispering in return. "You'll want to get out of here before canning season."

Amber grinned at the dire intonation.

"Sorry to bother you this late," Royce continued. "We've hired someone on to take care of the office while Jared and McQuestin are away." He gave Amber a wink, and something fluttered in her chest. She quickly picked up her wineglass to cover.

"She has some questions about the bank account. There have been a number of unpaid bills lately." He paused for a moment. "Why don't I let you talk to her directly?"

Amber hadn't expected that. She quickly swallowed and set down the glass. Good thing her questions were straightforward. She tucked her hair out of the way behind her ears, accepting the phone from Royce, ignoring the tingle when his fingers brushed hers.

"Hello?" she opened.

"Who am I speaking to?" asked Barry from the other end of the line.

"This is Amber, I'm—"

"And you're an employee at Ryder Ranch?" he asked directly.

She paused. "Uh, yes. That's right."

"Administrator? Bookkeeper?" There was an un-expected edge to the man's tone.

"Something like that." She gave Royce a confused look, and his eyes narrowed, crinkling slightly at the corners.

"Do you have a pen?" Barry asked, voice going even sharper.

"I—"

"Because you'd better write this down."

Amber glanced around at the countertops. "Just—"

"Sally Nettleton."

"Excuse me?"

"Sally Nettleton is the accounts supervisor. You can speak to her in the morning."

"Sure. Do you happen to have her—"

"And a warning, young lady. Don't you *ever* go above my head to Royce Ryder again."

Amber froze, voice going hollow. "What?"

"Share this conversation with him at your own peril. I don't tolerate insubordination, and he won't always be there to protect you."

Amber's mouth worked but sounds weren't coming out. Nobody had dared speak to her that way in her life.

"You're not the first, and you won't be the last. Don't fool yourself into thinking anything different." He stopped speaking, and the line fairly vibrated with tension.

She didn't know what to say. She had absolutely no idea what to tell this obnoxious man. Imagine if she really was an employee, dependent on her job. It would be horrible.

She heard a click and knew he'd signed off.

"Goodbye," she said weakly for the benefit of Royce and Stephanie.

"Told you he was feeling snarky today," said Stephanie.

"What did he say?" asked Royce. "You okay?"

"She looks a little pale," Stephanie put in.

"I'm fine," said Amber, debating with herself about what to tell Royce as she shut down the phone and handed it back.

"You didn't ask many questions," Royce ventured.

"He gave me a name. Sally Nettleton." She took a breath, framing her words carefully. "He was, well, annoyed that you'd put me in direct touch with him."

Royce frowned.

"He seems to think I broke the chain of command."

"So what?"

"I tell you, something's wrong with that man,"

Stephanie put in, dishing some of the crisp salad onto her plate.

Amber made up her mind, seeing little point in protecting Barry. In fact, she probably owed it to the rest of his staff to tell Royce the truth. "He seems to think I'm your lover."

It was Royce's turn to freeze. "He *said* that?"

"He said he didn't tolerate insubordination, and you won't always be around to protect me. That you'd lose interest."

A ruddy flush crept up Royce's neck, and he reached for his phone.

Amber put her hand over his. "Don't," she advised.

"Why the hell not?"

"Because he'll think you *are* protecting your lover."

"I don't give a rat's ass what—"

"Did I miss something?" asked Stephanie, glancing from one to the other, her tone laced with obvious anticipation and excitement. "Lovers?"

"No," they both shouted simultaneously.

"Too bad." She went back to her salad. "That would be cool."

Amber turned to Stephanie. "That would be tacky. You can't sleep with a man you've barely met." She silently commanded herself to pay close attention to those words.

"Sure you can," Stephanie chirped with a grin.

"No," Royce boomed at her. "You can't."

Stephanie giggled. "Good grief, you're an easy mark. There's nobody around here for me to sleep with anyway."

Some of the fight went out of Royce's posture, but his hand still gripped his phone.

Amber rubbed the tense hand. "Let it go."

"It's a firing offence."

"No, it's not."

"Yes, it is."

"At least give it some thought first." Barry had been a jerk, but she didn't want anyone getting fired on her account. "Maybe ask around. See if this was an isolated incident."

"He was rude to me this morning," said Stephanie.

"You're not helping," Amber warned.

Royce folded his arms across his chest. "It was *my* decision to call him directly. He doesn't get to second-guess me."

"Did you explain the circumstances?"

"I don't have to."

"So, he made an assumption. You can't fire a man for making an assumption."

He pasted her with a sharp look. "You like being spoken to that way."

"Of course not." But she'd like being Royce's lover. Heaven help her, she was pretty sure she'd like being Royce's lover.

Their gazes locked and held for a long moment, and she could have sworn he was reading her mind.

"The lasagna's getting cold," Stephanie pointed out conversationally.

Royce ended the moment with a sharp nod. "We'll talk about it later."

"Sure," Amber agreed, wondering if they were going to talk about Barry or about the energy that crackled between them like lightning.

Five

In Royce's mind, the issue was far from settled.

The storm had passed, leaving a bright moon behind. He closed the office door behind him for privacy, leaving Amber and Stephanie chatting out on the veranda, puppies scampering around them. He, on the other hand, flipped on the bright overhead light and crossed to the leather desk chair, snagging the desk phone and punching in Barry's home number.

It was nearly midnight in Chicago, but he didn't give a damn. Let the man wake up.

"Hello?" came a groggy, masculine voice.

"Barry?"

"Yes."

"It's Royce Ryder."

"Yes?" A shot of energy snapped into Barry's voice. "Anything wrong, Royce?"

There was plenty wrong. "Were you able to give Amber the information she needed?"

A pause. "I believe I did. Sally can cover anything else in the morning."

Royce waited a beat. "When I called you earlier, it wasn't because I wanted her to talk to Sally in the morning." Full stop. More silence.

"Oh. Well… I assumed—"

"Did you or did you not answer Amber's questions?" Royce repeated. And he could almost hear the wheels spinning inside Barry's head.

"I don't think you did," Royce said into the silence. "And the reason I don't think you did is because I was sitting right next to her during the call, and she didn't get a chance to ask you any questions." Once again, he stopped, giving Barry an opportunity to either contribute or sweat.

Hesitation was evident in the man's voice. "Did she… Mmm. Is she there?"

"No. She's not *here*. It's eleven o'clock. The woman's not working at eleven o'clock."

Silence.

"Here's my suggestion," said Royce. "To solve the problem. You hop on a plane in the morning. The corporate jet is unavailable, so you'll have to fly commercial. I'm thinking coach." He picked up an unopened envelope from the desktop and tapped it against the polished oak surface, dropping all pretence of geniality. "You get your ass to the ranch, and you apologize to Ms. Hutton. Then you answer any and all of her questions."

"I… But… Did you say Hutton?"

"David Hutton's daughter. But that couldn't matter less."

"Royce. I'm sorry. I didn't realize—"

"Apologize to *her.*"

"Of course."

"You'll be here tomorrow?"

"As soon as I can get there."

Satisfied, Royce disconnected. Amber only needed to be sure funds would be available in the account. But that wasn't the point anymore.

He gazed at the envelope in his hand. It was windowed. From North Pass Feed. Typical bill.

Curious after Amber's concern about his credit rating, he slit it open. Then he glanced through the other piles she'd made, arming himself with some basic information on the ranch expenses.

Half an hour later, he thought he had a picture of the accounts payable situation, so he headed back down the hallway to find Amber and Stephanie in the front foyer.

Stephanie was on her way out the door, and she gave him a quick kiss and a wave before piling into a pickup truck to head for home. As he closed the door behind her, the empty house seemed to hold its breath with anticipation.

Amber looked about as twitchy as he felt.

"You want to talk about Barry?" she asked, moving from the foyer into the great room.

"Taken care of," he answered, following a few paces behind her, letting his gaze trickle from her shoulders to her narrow waist, to her sexy rear end and the shapely thighs that were emphasized by her snug-fitting blue jeans.

She twisted her head. "What do you mean?"

"He'll be here in the morning."

She turned fully then. "I don't understand."

"He's coming by to apologize. And to answer your questions in person."

Her eyes widened in shock, red lips coming open in a way that was past sexy. "You didn't."

"He insisted."

"He did not."

Royce moved closer. "I suspect he understood the stakes."

She tipped her chin. "I don't need somebody to travel a thousand miles to offer me an insincere apology."

"But I do."

She didn't appear to have a comeback for that, and it was all he could do not to lean in for a kiss. She looked as if she wanted one. Her lips were full, eyes wide, body tipped slightly forward. If this was any other woman, at any other time...

But she'd made her position clear.

And he'd respect that.

Unless and until she told him otherwise.

Midday sun streaming through the ranch office window, Amber clicked through the headlines of a national news station on the office computer, reflecting with curiosity that she didn't feel out of touch with the rest of the world. She'd become a bit of a news junkie while finishing her degree, always on the lookout for emerging issues that might impact on her research. Having gone cold turkey in Montana, she should have missed watching world events unfold.

Of course, she had been a little distracted—okay, a

lot distracted by a sexy cowboy who was quickly making her forget there was a world outside the Ryder Ranch.

She'd half expected him to kiss her last night.

He'd stared down at her with those intense blue eyes, nostrils slightly flared, hands bunched into fists, and the muscles in his neck bulging in relief against his skin. She'd imagined him leaning down, planting his lips against hers, wrapping his arms around her and pulling her into paradise all over again.

But then he'd backed off, and she hadn't been brave enough to protest.

Now she sighed with regret as she clicked the mouse, bringing up a live news broadcast from a Chicago network. The buffer loaded, and the announcer carried on with a story about a local bridge repair.

She turned back to the desk, lifting the stack that was the day's mail. Barry Brewster hadn't arrived to confirm the bank balance yet, so she couldn't make any progress paying the backlog of bills.

Truth was, she was dreading the man's arrival. No matter what he said or did, it was going to be embarrassing all around. Royce might think she needed an apology, but Amber had spent most of her life with people being polite to her because they either admired or were afraid of her father or Hargrove. She didn't need the same thing from Barry today.

"The Governor's Office can no longer get away with dodging the issue of Chicago's competitiveness." The familiar voice startled Amber. She whirled to stare at the computer screen, where a news clip showed Hargrove posed in front of the Greenwood Financial Tower with several microphones picking up his words.

"His performance at the conference was shameful,"

Hargrove continued. "If our own governor won't stand up for the citizens of Chicago, I'd like to know who will."

Guilt percolated through Amber, and she quickly shut off the sound. She watched his face a few seconds longer, telling herself her actions had been defensible. If she'd stayed, she'd probably be standing right next him, holding his hand, the stalwart little fiancée struggling to come to terms with her role in his life.

He looked good on camera. Then, he'd always had a way with reporters, dodging their pointed questions without appearing rude, making a little information sound like a detailed dissertation. It was the reason the party was grooming him for the election.

A child shouted from outside the window, and Amber concentrated on the sound, forcing her mind from the worry about Hargrove to the seclusion of the ranch. Then another child shouted, and a chorus of cheers went up. Curious, she wandered to the window to look out.

Off to the left, on a flat expanse of lawn, a baseball game was underway. It was mostly kids of the ranch staff, but there were a few adults in the field. And there in the center, pitching the baseball, was Royce. She smiled when he took a few paces forward, lobbing a soft one to a girl who couldn't have been more than eight.

The girl swung and missed, but then she screwed her face up in defiance and positioned herself at the plate, tapping the bat on the white square in front of her. Royce took another step forward.

Amber smiled, then she glanced one more time at Hargrove on the computer screen—her old life.

As the days and hours had slipped by, she'd become more convinced that her decision was right. She had no intention of going back to her old life. And she owed it to Hargrove to make that clear.

She searched for her cell phone on the desktop, powered it up and dialed his number.

"Hargrove Alston," he answered.

"Hargrove? It's Amber."

Silence.

"I wanted to make sure you weren't worried about me," she began.

"I wasn't worried." His tone was crisp.

"Oh. Well, that's good. I'm glad."

"Your parents told me you were fine, and that you'd taken the trouble to contact them."

Amber clearly heard the "while you didn't bother to contact me" message underlying his words.

"Are you over your tantrum, then?" he asked.

She couldn't help but bristle. "Is that what you think I'm doing?"

"I think you're behaving like a child."

She gritted her teeth.

"You missed the Chamber of Commerce speech," he accused.

"I hear you didn't," she snarked in return.

Another silence. "And what is that supposed to mean?"

"Nothing."

"Honestly, Amber."

"Forget it. Of course you gave the speech. It was an important speech."

Her words seemed to mollify him. "Will you be ready in time for dinner, then? Flannigan's at eight with the Myers."

Amber blinked in amazement at the question.

She'd been gone for three days. She'd broken off their engagement.

"I'm not coming to dinner," she told him carefully.

He gave a heavy sigh on the other end of the phone. "Is this about the Switzerland trip?"

"Of course not."

"I explained why I had to go alone."

"This is about a fundamental concern with our compatibility as a couple."

"You sound like a self-help book."

Amber closed her eyes and counted to three. "I'm breaking our engagement, Hargrove. I'm truly sorry if I hurt you."

A flare of anger crept into his tone. "I wish you'd get over this mood."

"This isn't something I'm going to get over."

"Do you have any idea how embarrassing this could get?"

"I'm sorry about that, too. But we can't get married to keep from being embarrassed." She flicked a gaze to the baseball game, watching two colorful young figures dash around the bases.

"Are you trying to punish me?" asked Hargrove, frustration mounting in his tone. "Do you want me to apologize for…" He paused. "I don't know. Tell me what you think I've done?"

"You haven't done anything."

"Then get ready for dinner," he practically shouted.

"I'm not in Chicago."

He paused. "Where are you?"

"It doesn't—"

"Seriously, Amber. This is getting out of hand. I don't have time to play—"

"Goodbye, Hargrove."

"Don't you dare—"

She quickly tapped the end button then shut down the power on her phone. Talking around in circles wasn't going to get them anywhere.

She defiantly stuffed the phone into her pocket and drew a deep breath. After the tense conversation, the carefree baseball game was like a siren's call. Besides, it was nearly lunchtime, and she was tired of looking at numbers.

Determinedly shaking off her emotional reaction to the fight with Hargrove, she headed outside to watch.

Stephanie was standing at the sidelines.

"Looks like fun," said Amber, drawing alongside and opening the conversation. She inhaled the fresh air and let the cheerfulness of the crowd seep into her psyche.

"Usually it's just the kids," Stephanie told her. "But a lot of the hands are down from the range today, and Royce can't resist a game. And once he joined in, well…" She shrugged at the mixed-age crowd playing and watching.

A little girl made it to first, and a cocky, teenage boy swaggered up to the plate, reversing his baseball cap and pointing far out to right field with the tip of his bat.

Royce gave the kid an amused shake of his head, walked back to the mound and smacked the ball into the pocket of his worn glove. Then he shook his head in response to the catcher's hand signals. Royce waited, then smiled, and nodded his agreement to the next signal.

He drew back, bent his leg and delivered a sizzling fastball waist high and over the plate. The batter swung hard but missed. Royce chuckled, and the kid stepped out of the batter's box, adjusting his cap then scuffing his runners over the dirt at home plate.

"That's Robbie Nome," Stephanie informed her. "He's at that age, constantly challenging the hands."

"How old?" asked Amber, guessing sixteen or seventeen.

"Seventeen," Stephanie confirmed. "They usually settle down around eighteen. But there's a hellish year there in between while their brain catches up to their size and their testosterone level." She shook her head as Robbie swung and missed a second time.

"Royce seems pretty good," Amber observed, watching him line up for another pitch. She knew she was staring way too intently at him, but she couldn't help herself.

He was dressed in faded jeans, a steel-gray T-shirt and worn running shoes. His bare arms were deeply tanned, and his straight, white teeth shone with an infectious grin.

"He played in the College World Series."

"Pitcher?" asked Amber, impressed.

"First base."

Royce rocketed in a third pitch, and the batter struck out.

The outfielders let out a whoop and ran for the sidelines. The shoulders of the girl on first base slumped in dejection. Royce obviously noticed. He cut to her path, whispered something in her ear and ruffled her short, brown hair. She smiled, and he gave her a playful high five.

Then he spotted Amber and Stephanie, and made a beeline for them. Amber's chest contracted, and her heart lifted at the thought that his long strides were meant to bring him closer to her.

His gaze flicked to Stephanie but then settled back on Amber.

"Impressive," she complimented as he drew near.

He shrugged. "They're kids."

Stephanie held out her hand, and Royce smacked the glove into her palm. "You want to play?" she asked Amber.

Amber shook her head. "I need to get back to work." Then, as Stephanie trotted toward the outfield, she confided in Royce. "I've never been much of an athlete."

His gaze traveled her body. "Could've fooled me."

"Pilates and a StairMaster."

"I bet you'd be a natural at sports."

"We're not about to find out." She'd never swung a bat in her life. There were eight-year-olds out there who would probably show her up.

"I'd lob you a soft one," Royce offered, beneath the cheers and calls from the teams.

"Think I'll stick to bookkeeping."

He sobered. "You worked all morning?"

She nodded.

"Anything interesting?"

She shook her head. Actually, she'd found a couple of strange-looking payments in the computerized accounting system. But they were probably nothing, so she didn't want to bother Royce with that. And she sure wasn't about to tell him about her conversation with Hargrove.

"You surprise me," he said in an intimate tone.

"How so?"

"I had you pegged for a party girl."

"No kidding," she scoffed, rolling her eyes at his understatement.

"I didn't mean it that way."

She looked him straight on. "Yeah, you did."

He raked a hand through his sweat-damp hair, giving a sheepish smile. "Okay, I did for a while. But I got over it."

She paused, debating for a few silent seconds, but then deciding she was going to quit censoring herself. "So," she dared, with a toss of her hair. "What do you think of me now?"

His eyes danced, reflecting the color of the endless summer sky. "It could go one of two ways."

"Which are?"

"Royce!" someone called. "You're on deck."

He twisted his head to shout over his shoulder. "Be right there." Then he turned back, slowly contemplating her.

"Well?" she prompted, ridiculously apprehensive.

His hand came up to cup her chin, his thumb and forefinger warm against her skin. "You're either shockingly ingenuous or frighteningly cunning." But his tone took the sting out of the labels.

"Neither of those are complimentary," she pointed out, absorbing the sparks from his touch.

His tone went low. "But both are very sexy."

Then his hand dropped away, and he turned to the game, trotting toward the batter's box as a player took a base hit.

Amber skipped down the staircase, recalling Royce smacking a three-base hit, bringing ten-year-old Colby

Jones home to win the game by one run. She and Stephanie had decided to dress up for dinner, and she wore a white, spaghetti-strap cocktail dress and high-heeled sandals. She rounded the corner at the bottom of the stairs and caught sight of him in a pressed business suit. He was even sexier now than he'd been this afternoon in his T-shirt and jeans.

And he didn't look out of place in the rustic setting. She was glad she'd gone with the dress.

His gaze caught hers, dark and brooding, and she faltered on her high heels. This afternoon, he'd been almost playful. Had she done something to annoy him?

And then she caught sight of the second man, nearly as tall as Royce, somewhat thinner, his suit slightly wrinkled at the elbows and knees. The man turned at the sound of her footsteps, and she knew it had to be Barry Brewster. His jaw was tight, and beads of sweat had formed on his brow.

"Ms. Hutton," Royce intoned. "This is Barry Brewster. You spoke to him on the phone last night."

Amber fought an urge to laugh. The whole charade suddenly struck her as ridiculous. "Mr. Brewster," she said instead, keeping her face straight as she came to a stop and held out her hand.

"Barry, please."

"You can call me Amber."

"No, he can't."

"Royce, please."

But Royce didn't waver, shoulders square, expression stern.

"Ms. Hutton," Barry began, obviously not about to run afoul of his boss. "Please accept my apology. I was rude and insulting last night. I am, of course, available for anything you might need."

The irritation in his eyes belied the geniality of his tone. But then she hadn't expected him to be sincere about this.

"Thank you," she said simply. "I do have a couple of questions." She looked to Royce. "Should we sit down?"

"Unnecessary. Barry won't be staying."

"This is ridicul—"

Royce's hard expression shut her up, and she silently warned herself not to get on his bad side.

"I was hoping you could tell me the balance in the ranch bank account," she said to Barry. "There are a number of unpaid bills, so I wondered—"

"You don't need a reason to ask for the bank balance," Royce cut in.

"I'd need to look it up," said Barry, shifting from one black loafer to the other. He flexed his neck to one side and straightened the sleeves of his suit.

"So, look it up," said Royce.

"I don't have access to the server."

"Call someone who does."

Barry hesitated. "It's pretty late."

"Your point?"

"I guess I could try to catch Sally." With a final pause, Barry reached into his pocket for his phone.

While he dialed, Amber moved closer to Royce, turning her back on Barry.

"Is this completely necessary?" she hissed.

"I thought you wanted the bank balance."

"I do."

"Then it's completely necessary."

"You know that's not what I'm talking about."

"Let me handle this."

She took in the determined slant to Royce's chin while Barry's voice droned on in the background.

"Do I have a choice?" she asked.

"No."

"You can be a real hard-ass, you know that?"

"He insulted you."

"I'm a big girl. I'm over it."

"That's not the point."

She fought against a sudden grin at his need to get in the last word. "Do you ever give up?"

"No."

Barry cleared his throat, and Amber smoothly turned back to face him.

"Sally is looking into the overdraft and the line of credit to see where—"

"The balance," said Royce.

Barry's neck took on a ruddy hue, and he tugged at the white collar of his shirt. "It's, uh, complicated."

"I'm an intelligent man, and Amber has an honors degree."

Barry's gaze flicked to Amber, and she could have sworn she saw panic in its depths.

"I'd really rather discuss—"

"The balance," said Royce.

Barry drew a terse breath. "At the moment, the account is overdrawn."

There were ten full seconds of frozen silence.

Stephanie entered the room from the kitchen, stopping short as she took in the trio.

"Say again?" Royce widened his stance.

"There's been... That is..." This time when Barry

glanced at Amber, he seemed to be pleading for help. There was no help she could give him. She didn't have a clue what was going on.

Royce's voice went dangerously low. "Why didn't you transfer something from corporate?"

Barry tugged at his collar again. "The China deal."

"What about the China deal?" Royce asked carefully. "Was the transfer held up?"

Barry swallowed, his Adam's apple bobbing, voice turning to a raspy squeak. "The paperwork. From Cheng Li. It didn't make the deadline."

Stephanie's eyes went wide, while Royce cocked his head, brows creasing. "They assured me the fax would go through."

"It did. But...well..."

Royce crossed his arms over his chest.

"Our acknowledgment," said Barry. "The time zone difference."

"You didn't send the acknowledgment?"

"End of day. Chicago time."

"You missed the deadline?" Royce's voice was harsh with disbelief.

"I've been trying to fix it for thirty-six hours."

Royce took a step forward. "You *missed* a fifty-million-dollar deadline?"

Barry's mouth opened, but nothing came out.

"And you didn't call me?" Royce's voice was incredulous now.

"I was trying to fix—"

"Yesterday," Royce all but shouted, index finger jabbing in Barry's direction. "*Yesterday,* I could have called Jared at his hotel. Today, he's on a sailboat somewhere in the South Pacific. You have..." Royce raked a hand through his hair. "I don't even know how much money you've lost."

"I—"

"What in the *hell* happened?"

"It was the time zones. Technology. The language barrier."

"You are *so* fired."

Amber's gaze caught Stephanie's. She felt desperate for an exit. She didn't want to witness Royce's anger, Barry's humiliation. She wanted to be far, far away from this disturbing situation.

"You're done, Barry," Royce confirmed to the silent man.

Barry hesitated a beat longer. Then his shoulders dropped. The fight went out of him, and he turned for the door.

The room seemed to boom with silence as Barry's footsteps receded and the car pulled away outside.

Stephanie took a few hesitant steps toward her brother. "Royce?"

"Cancel his credit cards," Royce commanded. "Wake up someone from IT and change the computer passwords. And have security reset the codes on the building."

"What are we going to do?" Stephanie asked in a whisper.

Royce's hands curled into fists at his sides. He looked to Amber. "I have to call Beijing. If we don't fix this, the domino effect could be catastrophic."

Amber nodded. "Just tell me what you need."

"Can we talk to Jared?" asked Stephanie.

Royce shook his head. "Not a chance. Not for a week at least."

Six

Amber hung up the phone after their fifth call to China, her expression somber as Royce's mood.

"That's it." He voiced his defeat out loud.

"Are you sure?"

"Can you think of anything else?"

She shook her head.

He slipped the phone from her hands, setting it on the end table next to the sofa in the living room. The deadline was the deadline, and they hadn't been able to penetrate the Chinese bureaucracy to make their case to Cheng Li. The deal was canceled.

It was nearly 3:00 a.m. Only a few lights burned in the house, and Stephanie had headed to her own ranch an hour ago. Amber tipped her head back on the gold sofa cushion, closing her eyes. She'd struggled through translations for hours on end, and the strain was showing in her pale complexion.

Royce gave in to the temptation to smooth a lock of hair from her cheek. "You okay?"

"Just sorry I couldn't help."

He dropped his hand back down. "You did help."

She opened her eyes. "How so?"

"I understand now what is and isn't possible."

"Nothing's possible."

"Apparently not."

She blinked her dark lashes, and her hand covered his. "How bad is it?"

He rested his own head against the sofa back. "It'll play havoc with our cash flow. We may have to sell off some of our companies. But, to start off, I'm going to have to call the division heads to keep them from panicking. Firing Barry was a significant move."

"Will they be angry?"

He shrugged. "That's the least of my worries."

Amber didn't answer, and Royce was content to sit in silence. He turned his hand, palm up, wrapping it around her smaller one. For some reason, it gave him comfort. Simply sitting here quietly, with her by his side, made the problems seem less daunting.

Her hand went limp in his, and he turned to gaze at her closed eyes and even breathing. She was astonishingly beautiful—smooth skin, delicate nose, high cheekbones and lustrous, golden hair that made a man want to bury his face against it.

He felt a shot of pity for the hapless Hargrove. Imagine having Amber in your grasp then having her disappear? Not that the man wasn't better off. Royce glanced at the portrait of his parents on their wedding day. He usually put it away while he was at the ranch, unable to bear the look of unbridled adoration on his father's face.

And that's the way it would have been with Amber, too. Her husband would have gone completely stupid and helpless with longing, only to have her change her mind and move on. Poor, pathetic Hargrove. He wouldn't have known what hit him.

Royce extricated his hand from hers, shifting to the edge of the couch, positioning himself to lift her into his arms.

"Amber?" he whispered softly, sliding one arm around her back and the other beneath her knees.

She mumbled something unintelligible, but her head tipped to rest against his shoulder. He lifted her up, and she stayed sleeping, even as he adjusted her slight body in his arms.

She weighed less than nothing. She was also soft and her scent appealing. There was something completely right about the scent of a beautiful woman, particularly this beautiful woman, fresh, like wildflowers, he supposed, but sweeter, more compelling.

He moved his nose toward her hair, guessing it was her shampoo. Hard to tell, really. He mounted the staircase, taking his time, reluctant to arrive at her room where he'd have to put her down.

His imagination wandered to that moment. Should he help her undress? Slip her between the sheets in her underwear? Would a gentleman wake her up or leave her in her clothes? Never having been a gentleman, Royce wasn't sure.

This had to be the first time he'd put a woman to bed without immediate plans to join her. He couldn't help a self-deprecating smile. It figured. He also couldn't remember a moment in his life when he'd been more eager to join a woman in bed.

He pushed open her door, carefully easing her through the opening. Then he crossed to the queen-size, brass bed and leaned down, laying her gently on top of the comforter.

She moaned her contentment, and his longing ratcheted up a notch. Their faces were only inches apart, his arm around her back, the other cradling her bare legs. He knew he had to leave her, but try as he might, he couldn't get his body to cooperate.

"Amber," he whispered again, knowing that if she woke he'd have no choice but to walk away.

"Mmm," she moaned. Then she sighed and wriggled in his arms.

His muscles tensed to iron. His gaze took in her pouty lips and, before he knew it, his head was dipping toward hers. Then he was kissing her sweet lips.

Just to say good-night, he promised himself. Just a chaste—

But then she was kissing back.

Her arms twined around his neck, and her head tipped sideways, lips parting, accommodating his ravenous kiss. Her back arched, and her fingertips curled into his short hair, even as her delicate tongue flicked into his mouth.

He leaned into her soft breasts, stroking the length of her bare legs, teasing the delicate skin behind her knees, tracing the outline of her shapely calves and daring the heat of her smooth thighs.

He wanted her, more than he'd ever wanted a woman in his life. Passion was quickly clouding reason, and his hormones warred with intelligence. Another minute, another second, and his logic would switch completely off.

He dragged his mouth from hers. "Amber?" he forced himself to ask. "Are you sure you're ready for this?"

Her eyes popped open, and she took a sudden jerk back against the pillow. She blinked in confusion at Royce's face, and in a split and horrible second, he realized what had happened.

The woman had been dreaming.

And Royce wasn't the man she'd been dreaming about.

In the morning, Amber was grateful to find Stephanie in the kitchen at breakfast. She needed a buffer between her and Royce while she got over her embarrassment.

She'd hesitated a moment too long last night. When she'd realized it wasn't a dream, she should have kept right on kissing him. She should have pressed her body tightly against his and sent the signal that she was completely attracted to him, nearly breathless with passion for him, and that making love was exactly what she wanted.

Instead, all he'd seen was her shock and hesitation. He'd been offended and abruptly left the room. She didn't blame him. And she wasn't brave enough to try to explain.

"Morning, Amber." Stephanie was her usual bright self as she bit into a strip of bacon, legs swinging from the high chair at the breakfast bar.

"Morning," Amber replied, daring a fleeting glance at Royce.

He gave her a cool nod then turned his attention

back to Stephanie. "Two days at the most," he told Stephanie.

"I'll definitely get you something," she responded and blew out a sigh. "This is the worst possible time."

"I can't imagine there being a best possible time." Royce stood from the breakfast bar and carried his plate and coffee mug over to the sink. He downed the last of the coffee before setting everything on the counter.

Amber helped herself to a clean plate from the cupboard and took a slice of toast from the platter.

"Royce has to call a division heads meeting," Stephanie told her. "We need to ask for financial reports from everybody. But he's worried about panic."

"Who would panic?" Amber addressed her question first to Royce, but when he didn't meet her eyes, she turned back to Stephanie.

"I need a pretext for the meeting," said Royce. "Barry Brewster's firing is bad enough. Add to that a sudden meeting and financial reports, and the gossip will swirl.

"We have over two thousand employees," he continued. "Some very big contracts, and some very twitchy clients." His gaze finally went to Amber, but his face remained impassive, his tone flat. "If you don't mind, we'll start a rumor you were the cause."

"You mean the cause of Barry Brewster being fired, not the money problems?"

Royce didn't react to her joke. "Yes."

"Are you leaving today?" asked Stephanie.

At first Amber thought Stephanie meant her, and the idea made her clench her stomach in regret. But then she realized Stephanie was talking to her brother.

Royce nodded.

"Where—" Amber clamped her jaw to slow herself down. It was jarring to think of him leaving with this tension between them. "Where are you going?" she finished, feigning only a mild interest.

"Chicago."

"You don't think that will bring on the gossip?"

She assured herself her caution was sincere. It wasn't merely an attempt to keep Royce here at the ranch.

His eyes narrowed.

"If you come rolling into the office, people are sure to think something's up."

"She's right," Stephanie put in.

"I don't see an alternative. I have to talk to the division VPs."

"Bring them here," suggested Amber.

Both Royce and Stephanie stared at her.

"There's your pretext. Come up with a reason to bring them here. Something fun, something frivolous, then take them aside and have whatever discreet conversation you need to have." She paused, but neither of them jumped in.

"A barbecue." She offered the first thing that popped into her mind.

Royce's voice turned incredulous, but at least there was an emotion in it. "You want me to fly the Ryder senior managers to Montana for a barbecue?"

"They'd never suspect," she told him.

"A barn dance," Stephanie cried, coming erect on the seat. "We'll throw a dance to christen the new barn."

"You're both insane," Royce grumbled.

"Like a fox," said Stephanie. "Invite the spouses. Hire a band. Nobody throws a dance and barbecue when the company's in financial trouble."

Amber waited. So did Stephanie.

Royce's brows went up, and his mouth thinned out. "I find I can't disagree with that statement."

Finished with her own breakfast, Stephanie hopped up and transferred her dishes to the sink. She gave Royce a quick peck on the cheek. "See you guys in a while. I have to get the students started."

As she left the room, Amber screwed up her courage. She definitely needed to clear the air. "Royce—"

"If you have time today," he interrupted, "could you give me as much information as possible on the cattle ranch finances?" His voice was detached, professional, and his gaze seemed to focus on her hairline.

Amber hated the cold wall between them. "I…"

"Stephanie's going to pull something together for the horse operation, and I'll be busy—"

"Of course," Amber quickly put in, swallowing, telling herself she had no right to feel hurt. "Whatever you need."

He gave a sharp nod. "Thanks. Appreciate you helping out." Then he turned and strode out of the kitchen, boot heels echoing on the tile floor.

Amber was curled up on the webbed cushions of an outdoor love seat on the ranch house deck, clouds slipping over the distant mountains, making mottled shade on the nearby aspen groves. She flipped her way through a hundred-page printout from the ranch's financial system, highlighting entries along the way.

Gopher, one of Molly's young pups, had curled up against her bare feet. At first, she'd been wary of his wet nose and slurpy tongue. But then he'd fallen asleep, and she found his rhythmic breathing and steady heartbeat rather comforting.

She hadn't seen Royce since breakfast, and Stephanie was obviously busy getting her own financial records together. Amber's thoughts had vacillated from heading straight for home, to confronting Royce about last night, to seducing Royce, to helping him sort out his business problems and earning his gratitude.

She sighed and let her vision blur against the page. For the hundredth time, she contemplated her mistake. Why had she panicked last night? Why hadn't she kissed him harder, hugged him tighter and waited to see where it would all lead?

She was wildly attracted to him. She was truly free from Hargrove now, and there was no reason in the world she couldn't follow her desires. So what if she'd only known him a few days? They were both adults, and this was hardly the 1950s.

Gopher shifted his warm little body, reminding her of where she was and that, 1950s or not, she'd blown her chance with Royce. The choices left were to leave him, seduce him or impress him. Since she was completely intimidated by the thought of seducing a man she'd already rebuffed, she decided to go with impressing him.

She forced herself to focus on the column of numbers in her lap.

There it was again.

She stroked the highlighter across the page.

Yet another payment to Sagittarius Eclipse Incorporated. It was for one hundred thousand dollars, just like the last one, and the one before that.

She skipped back on the pages, counting the payments

and pinpointing the dates of the transactions. They fell on the first day of every month. Where other payments in the financial report were for obvious things like feed, lumber, tools or veterinary services, the Sagittarius Eclipse payments were notated only as "services."

Amber's curiosity was piqued. She flipped to the back page. Scanning through the total columns, she discovered one-point-two million dollars had been paid out to Sagittarius Eclipse in the current year, the same amount the year before.

She pulled her feet from the love seat cushion. Gopher whimpered and quickly scooted up next to her thigh, flopping against her.

She smiled at the little puff ball, set the financial report aside and scooped him into her arms. He wiggled for a moment, but then settled in next to her like a fuzzy baby.

"I suppose if I hold on to you, you can't do any harm," she whispered to him, checking Molly and the other pups as she rose to her feet. They were curled together at the far end of the deck. Nobody seemed to notice as she carried Gopher through the doorway.

There was a computer close by in the living room, and she sat down in front of it, moving the mouse to bring the screen back to life. She hadn't graduated in Public Administration without knowing how to search a company. Using her free hand, she called up a favorite corporate registry search program.

An hour later, she knew nothing, absolutely nothing about Sagittarius Eclipse Incorporated. They had to be an offshore company, and a hard-to-trace one at that. She could hear her father's voice inside her head, warning her that when something didn't seem right, something definitely wasn't right. But since she wasn't nearly as suspicious as her father, she refused to jump to any conclusions.

Shifting the sleeping puppy, she dug into her pocket to retrieve her cell phone, dialing Stephanie's number.

"Yo!" came the young woman's voice.

"It's Amber."

"I know. What's going on?"

"You ever heard of a company called Sagittarius Eclipse?"

"Who?"

Amber repeated the name.

"What are they, astrologers or something?"

"I hope not." Amber nearly chuckled. If Ryder Ranch was paying for a hundred grand a month of astrology services, they'd better be accurately predicting the stock market.

"Never heard of them," said Stephanie. "How are things looking at your end?"

"Best I can come up with is to stop work on the new barn," said Amber. And maybe quit paying for unidentified "services." But something stopped her from mentioning the strange payments to Stephanie.

"I hate to say it," Stephanie returned, "but I'd better not buy Blanchard's Run."

"I thought that was a foregone conclusion."

"A girl can hope."

This time, Amber did laugh at the forlorn little sigh in Stephanie's voice. "Suck it up, princess."

"Easy for you to say. It's not your business being compromised."

Amber couldn't deny it. What's more, she couldn't ignore the fact that she didn't have a business to compromise. Nor did she have a career to compromise. The only thing she'd ever been able to call a vocation was her role as Hargrove's loyal fiancée and future wife. And she'd completely blown that job yesterday.

"What else have you got?" she asked, shoving the disagreeable thoughts to the back of her mind.

"Let me see." Stephanie shuffled some papers in the background. "I can delay a tack order, struggle through with our existing jumps. Man, I hate to do that. But the horses have to eat, the employees need paychecks, and we don't dare cut back on the competition schedule."

Royce's deep voice broke in from behind Amber. "I see you've changed your mind."

She jerked around to face him in his Western shirt and faded jeans. A flush heated her face. Yes, she'd changed her mind. She'd changed her mind the second he left her bedroom last night.

But he was staring at the puppy in her lap, and she realized he was referring to a completely different subject.

"Royce is here," she said into the mouthpiece.

"Tell him I'll be down there before dinner."

"Sure." She signed off and hung up the phone, adjusting Gopher's little body when she realized her arm was beginning to tingle from lack of circulation. "He's very friendly," she told Royce.

"Are you taking him home?"

"Have you ever heard of a company called Sagittarius Eclipse?" she countered, not wanting to open the subject of her going home. She'd pretend she didn't notice he was anxious for her to leave.

"Never," he answered, watching her closely, the

distance and detachment still there in his expression and stance.

She debated her next move, unable to shake the instinct that told her the payments were suspicious.

"Why do you ask?" he prompted.

"The ranch is making payments to them."

"For what?"

"That's just it. I can't tell."

"Tools? Supplies? Insurance?"

"Insurance, maybe." She hadn't thought of that. "The entries only say 'services.'" She reached behind her for the report, and Gopher wriggled in her lap.

"Better put him back outside," Royce suggested.

Amber moved to the screen door, deposited the puppy on the deck and returned to point out the entries to Royce.

"I searched for the company on the Internet," she offered while he glanced through the pages she'd noted. "I can't find anything on them, not domestically, not offshore."

He raised a questioning brow.

"I learned corporate research at U of C."

Royce's jaw tightened, and she could feel the wheels turning inside his head.

She dared voice the suspicion that was planted inside her brain. "Do you think McQuestin could be—"

"No."

"His niece?"

"Not a chance. Not for these amounts."

"McQuestin had to know, right?" The man worked with the business accounts on a daily basis. Whatever was going on with Sagittarius Eclipse, McQuestin had to be aware.

"It's legit," Royce said out loud, but his spine was stiff, and he was frowning.

"What do you want to do?" she asked. Maybe this was the tip of the iceberg. Maybe Sagittarius Eclipse would help them solve some kind of embezzlement scheme. Maybe she could even help alleviate the company's cash flow problems.

He reached into the breast pocket of his blue-and-gray plaid shirt, retrieving his cell phone and searching for a number. His hair was damp with sweat, face streaked with dust, sleeves rolled up to reveal his tanned, muscular forearms. Amber's gaze went on a wayward tour down his body, her hormones reaching with predictability to his sex appeal.

He pressed a button on the phone, and the ringing tone became audible through the small speaker.

Amber pointed to the screen door. "Do you want me to—"

Royce shook his head. "You're the one that found it. Let's hear what McQuestin has to say."

A woman's voice bid them hello.

"Maddy? It's Royce."

"Oh, hey, Royce. He's doing okay today. They think they got the last of the bone fragments, and the infection's calming down."

"Good to hear," said Royce. "Can I talk to him for a minute?"

Maddy hesitated. "He's pretty doped up. Can I help with something?"

"It's important," said Royce, an apology in his voice.

"Well. Okay." The sounds went muffled for a few moments.

"Yeah?" came a gravelly voice.

"It's Royce, Mac. How're you feeling?"

"Like the bronc won," McQuestin grumbled.

Amber couldn't help but smile.

"You married yet?" McQuestin's voice was slightly slurred.

"That was Jared," Royce corrected.

"Mighty pretty girl," McQuestin mused. "Should have married her yourself."

"Jared might have had an objection to that."

"He's too busy… Hey! Did you wash the ears?"

Royce and Amber glanced at each other in amusement.

"Mac," Royce tried.

"What now?" MacQuestin grumbled.

"You know anything about Sagittarius Eclipse?"

There was a silence, during which their amusement turned to concern.

"I paid 'em," said McQuestin, obviously angry. "What else would a man do?"

"What exactly did you pay them for?"

McQuestin snorted. "You tell Benteen…" Then his voice turned to a growl. "Somebody should have shot the damn dog yesterday."

Maddy's voice came back. "Can this wait, Royce? You're really upsetting him."

"I'm sorry, Maddy. Of course it can wait. Keep me posted, okay?"

"Will do." McQuestin's voice still ebbed and flowed in the background. "Better go."

Royce signed off.

"Who's Benteen?" asked Amber.

Royce's voice was thoughtful, and he placed the phone

back in his pocket. "My grandfather. He died earlier this year. You think you could dig a little deeper into this?"

Amber nodded. Her curiosity was piqued. She'd like nothing better than to sleuth around Sagittarius Eclipse and figure out its relationship to the Ryder Ranch.

Seven

"Royce?"

Royce's body reacted to the sound of Amber's voice. He hefted a hay bale onto the stack, positioning it correctly before acknowledging her presence.

"Yeah?" He didn't turn to look at her. It was easier for him to cope if only one of his senses was engaged with her at a time. He only hoped she'd keep her sweet scent on the far side of the barn.

Her footsteps echoed. So much for that plan.

"I didn't find any more information," she said. "I'm going to have to try again tomorrow."

He nodded, moving to the truckload of hay bales, keeping his gaze fixed on his objective.

"It's getting late," she ventured, and there was a vulnerability in her voice that made his predicament even worse. Though he didn't look at her now, an image

of her this afternoon, in that short denim skirt, a peach
tank top, her blond hair cascading softly around her bare
shoulders, was stuck deep in the base of his brain. It was
going to take dynamite to blast it out.

"I know." He gave the short answer.

"What are you doing?"

He grabbed the next bale, binder twine pressing
against the reinforced palms of his leather work gloves.
"Moving hay bales."

He retraced his steps. Extreme physical work was
his only hope of getting any sleep tonight. If he wasn't
dead-dog exhausted, he'd do nothing but lie awake and
think about Amber sleeping across the hall.

"Is it that important?" she pressed.

"Horses have to eat."

"But do you—"

"Is there something you need?" he asked brusquely.

Her silence echoed between them, and he felt like a
heel.

"No," she finally answered in a soft voice. "It's
just…"

He didn't prompt her, hoping she'd take the hint and
leave. He'd never found himself so intensely attracted
to a woman, and it was physically painful to fight it.

"I'm surprised is all," she continued.

He mentally rolled his eyes. Couldn't the woman take
a hint? Did she like that she was making him crazy?
Was she one of those teases that got her jollies out of
tempting a man then turning up her prissy little nose at
his advances?

"When you said you had to babysit the ranch—"

How the hell long was she going to keep this up?

"—I thought you meant in a more managerial sense. I mean, can't somebody else move the hay?"

He turned to look at her then. Damn it, she was still wearing that sexy outfit. Only it was worse now, because the cool evening air had hardened her nipples, and they were highlighted against the soft cotton where she stood in the pool of overhead light.

The air whooshed right out of his lungs, and he almost dropped the bale.

"I'd rather do it myself," he finally ground out.

"I see." She held his gaze. There was something soft in the depths of her eyes, something warm and welcoming.

At this very second, he could swear she was attracted to him. But he'd been down that road before. Down that road was a long night in a very lonely bed.

He went back to work.

"Royce?" Her footsteps echoed again as she moved closer.

He heaved the bale into place, gritted his teeth and turned. "What?" he barked.

"I'm…" She glanced at the scuffed floor. "Uh… sorry."

He swiped his forearm across his sweaty brow. "Not as sorry as I am."

She glanced up in confusion. "For what? What did you do?"

"I didn't *do* anything."

"Then, what do you have to be sorry about?"

"You want to know why I'm sorry?" He'd reached the breaking point, and he was ready to give it to her with both barrels. "You really want to know why I'm sorry?"

She gave a tentative nod.

"I'm sorry I walked into the Ritz-Carlton lounge."

Her eyes widened as he stripped off his gloves.

"And I'm sorry I brought you home with me." He tossed the gloves on the nearest hay bale. "And I'm sorry you're so beautiful and desirable and sexy. But mostly, *mostly* I'm sorry my family's future is falling down around my ears, and all I can think of is how much I want you."

Their eyes locked.

For a split second, it looked as though she smiled.

"You think this is *funny?*"

She shook her head. Then she took a step forward. "I think it's ironic."

"You might not want to get too close," he warned, drinking in the sight, sound and scent of her all in one shot, wondering how many seconds he could hold out before he dragged her into his arms.

"Yeah?" She stepped closer still.

"Did you not hear me?"

She placed her flat palm against his chest. "I heard you just fine." Her defiant blue eyes held one of the most blatant invitations he'd ever seen.

He hoped she knew what she was doing.

Hell, who was he kidding? He couldn't care less if she knew or not. Just so long as she didn't back off this time.

His arms went around her and jerked her flush against him, all but daring her to protest.

Then he bent his head; his desire and frustration transmitted themselves into a powerful kiss. He all but devoured her mouth, reveling in the feel of her thighs, belly and breasts, all plastered against his aching flesh.

He encircled her waist, pulling in at the small of her back, bending her backward, kissing deeper as his free hand strummed from hip to waist over her rib cage to capture the soft mound of her breast.

She groaned against his mouth, lips parting farther, her tongue answering the impassioned thrusts of his own. Her nipple swelled under his caress, fueling his desire and obliterating everything else from his brain. He bent his knee, shifting his thigh between hers, pushing up on her short skirt, settling against the silk of her panties.

Her hands gripped his upper arms, nails scraping erotically against his thin shirt, transmitting her passion to the nerves of his skin. He lifted her, spreading her legs, hands cupping her bottom, shoving the skirt out of the way and pressing her heat against him.

Her arms went around his neck, legs tightening, her lips hot on his, her silky hair flowing out in all directions around her shoulders. She braced her arms on his shoulders, fingers delving into his short hair. Her kisses moved from his mouth to his cheek, his chin and his neck. She tugged at the buttons of his shirt, loosening them, before dipping her head and trailing her kisses across his chest.

He tipped back his head, drinking in the heat and moisture of her amazing lips. Then he took a few steps sideways, behind the bale stack, screening them from the rest of the cavernous room. He shrugged out of his loose shirt, dropping it on a bale before settling her on top. He braced his arms on either side of her and pulled back to look.

Her eyes were closed, lips swollen red. Her chest

heaved with labored breaths, and his gaze settled on the outline of her breasts against the peach top.

"Royce?"

His name on her lips tightened his chest and sent a fresh wave of desire cascading through his veins. He swiftly stripped her top off over her head, revealing two perfect breasts peeking from a lacy, white bra that dipped low in the center and barely camouflaged her dusky nipples.

"Gorgeous," he breathed, popping the clasp and letting the wisp of fabric fall away. "Perfection."

Her lash-fringed lids came up, revealing blue eyes clouded with passion.

They stared at each other for a long suspended breath. Then he reached out, his tanned hand dark against her creamy breast. He stroked the pad of his thumb across her nipple.

She gasped, and he smiled in pure satisfaction.

He repeated the motion, and she grabbed for his waist, tugging him toward her. But he stood his ground, his gaze flicking to the shadow of her sheer, high-cut panties, the skirt pulled high to reveal her hips.

He traced the line of elastic, knuckle grazing the moist silk. She moaned, head tipping back against the golden hay, her arms falling to her sides, clenching her fists tightly.

He could feel his anticipation, his own blood singing insistently through his system, hormones revving up, his passion making demands on his brain. But he wasn't ready. He wasn't ready to let the roar toward completion hijack his senses.

While his fingertips roamed, he leaned forward,

taking one plump nipple into his mouth, curling his tongue around the exquisite texture.

A deep sound burbled in Amber's throat, and her hands went for his belt buckle, the snap of his jeans, his zipper, his boxers, and then he was in her hand, and he knew time was running out.

He hooked his thumbs over the sides of her panties, stripping them down, letting them drop to the floor. Then his body moved unerringly to hers.

Her legs wrapped around his waist, and he raised his head, gazing into her eyes as he flexed his hips, easing slowly as he could to her center and into her core. Her eyes widened with every inch, she clenched her hands on his hips, and her sweet mouth fell open in a pout of awe.

Unable to resist, he bent his head, her features blurred as he grew close. Then her mouth opened against his, and his tongue thrust in, mimicking the motions of his hips as nature took over and he let the primal rhythm throb free between them.

He cupped her face, caressed her hair, kissed her neck, her temple, her eyelids. His hands roamed free, stroking her thighs, her bottom, her belly and breasts. Her panting breaths were music to his ears, her nails crescenting into his back transmitted her fervor.

Then she cried his name, urging him on, playing havoc with his self-control. But she was with him, and the small tremors contracting her body catapulted him over the edge into oblivion.

Amber blinked open her eyes.

She was vaguely aware of hay strands tickling her bare back. But she was much more aware of Royce's hard, hot body engulfing her own. Her lungs were struggling to get enough oxygen, and every fiber of her muscles danced with the aftershocks of lovemaking.

Royce's palm stroked over her hair, and he kissed her eyelids. Despite her exhaustion, her lips curled into a smile. But she was a long way from being able to speak.

Her skirt was in a bunch around her waist, her other clothes scattered. Her hair was wild and disheveled, tangled with hay, while her lips tingled with the heat of his kisses.

"I don't know what to say," Royce whispered in her ear.

She struggled through a few more breaths. "Well, I'm definitely not sorry," she managed, and she heard him chuckle.

"Definitely not sorry," he echoed.

He eased back, taking in her appearance.

"Bad?" she asked.

He pulled some straw from her hair. "Telltale."

She raked spread fingers through her hair in an attempt to tame it while he refastened his jeans.

He bent and picked up her bra from the floor, frowned at the dirt streaks on it and tucked it into his back pocket. He located her tank top, gave her breasts one last, lingering look, then pulled her top back over her head. The peach color was blotted with dust. And Royce's attempts to brush it off made things worse.

"We'll probably want to sneak you in the back way," he joked as she tugged down her skirt. He watched her movements closely.

She slipped his wrinkled shirt from beneath her butt

and held it out to him. "You're not looking so sharp yourself, cowboy."

"I've been working hard." As he shrugged into his shirt, his gaze strayed from the top of her head to the tips of her toes, and his tone went soft and intimate. "What's your excuse?"

"Someone stole my underwear."

He reached for the wisp of silk caught on the side of a bale and tucked it into his pocket with her bra.

"That's my only pair."

"Yeah?" He gave her body another long look. "Lucky me."

He fastened his buttons then helped her down, tucking her hand in his as they headed across the barn. "I hope you know you're sleeping in my bed tonight."

"Only if you give my underwear back."

"Maybe."

"Maybe?"

He turned to gaze at her. "Talk me into it."

Her footsteps slowed, and so did his. With their joined hands, he reeled her in, then he smoothed her hair back once more, moving closer still, voice intimate. "You know, you are stunningly gorgeous."

A smile tickled the corners of her mouth. "Is that why you're sneaking me in the back way?"

"I'm keeping you all to myself," he whispered, lips coming down on hers.

The kiss nearly exploded between them. For all that they'd just made love, Amber's arousal was strong as ever. She wrapped her arms around his neck, came up on her toes, welcomed his tongue and reveled in the feel of his warm hands as they stroked over her back, across her buttocks, down her thighs, then back up beneath her skirt.

She pressed her body against his as the kiss went on and on. A groan slipped from her lips.

"Again?" he asked, voice husky.

She nodded.

"Here or in bed."

"I don't care." She truly didn't. Royce could make her body sing, and propriety didn't appear to have a lot to do with it.

He backed off slightly on the kiss and smoothed her skirt back down. "In bed."

"Really?"

He grinned at the disappointment in her tone. "I want to make love to you for a very, very long time."

She cocked her head sideways. "And you need a bed for that?"

"I don't plan to be able to move afterward."

She breathed a mock, drawn-out sigh. "If you think I'll wear you out..."

"Is that a challenge?"

She gave a teasing half smile and rapidly blinked her lashes.

In return, he planted a playful swat on her buttocks. "You're on, sweetheart."

Amber stifled a yawn in the bright, midday sunshine, stretching her taut thigh muscles as she leaned on the railing of the ranch house deck. The puppies were below, chasing each other and rolling around on the meadow that sloped toward the river. Off the end of the deck, Amber could see the ranch hands putting up five giant tents in preparation for Saturday's barbecue and barn dance.

She was dividing her time between the Sagittarius Eclipse mystery and the barbecue. She'd never planned an event quite like this before. They'd hired a local band. Hamburgers and hot dogs were making up the main course, while salads, potato chips and condiments seemed to round out the rest. They had plans for a giant cake for dessert, with papers plates, soft drinks and canned beer all around.

Amber wasn't sure how the Ryder International executives would react to the dinner, though she was sure their kids would love the wagon rides, horseshoes and baseball game Stephanie had planned. When she'd broached the possibility of steaks, wine and real china with Sasha, the woman looked at her as though she'd lost her mind.

Okay, so they did corporate entertaining a little differently here in Montana. Amber could conform. And at least the event wasn't likely to damage the Ryder International bottom line.

Tucking her windblown hair behind one ear, she pressed the on button of her cell phone, and dialed Katie's work number.

"Katie Merrick," came the familiar voice.

"It's Amber."

"What? Finally! Have you gone stark raving mad?"

"You've been talking to my mom, haven't you?"

"Of course I've been talking to your mom. And your dad. And Hargrove. You've got him completely confused."

"I thought I cleared up the confusion yesterday."

"By breaking it off over the phone?" The accusation was clear in Katie's tone.

"I'm a little ways away, Katie."

"Where?"

Amber scratched her fingernail over a dried flower petal the rain had stuck to the painted railing, deciding she couldn't keep it a secret forever. "Montana."

Silence.

"Katie?"

"Did you say Montana?"

"Yes. I'm staying with a…well, friend. I need your help with something."

"I'd say you need a whole lot more than *my* help. The dress arrived yesterday."

"What dress?"

"Your *wedding* dress." Katie's voice was incredulous. "The one from Paris. The one with antique alençon lace and a thousand hand-sewn pearls."

"Oh." Right. That dress. Amber supposed they'd have to put it on consignment somewhere. "The thing I wanted to talk to you about at the moment, though, was business."

"What do you mean?"

"I have a problem."

"What problem?" Katie's voice immediately turned professional.

"It's a company called Sagittarius Eclipse. I haven't been able to trace it, but I think it's got to be offshore somewhere, maybe hiding behind a numbered company. It could be connected to embezzlement."

There was another moment's silence. "Where did you say you were?" asked Katie.

Amber drew a sigh. "You remember that thirty dollars I gave you last week?"

"To pay for the dry cleaning on my dress?"

"You're on retainer, Katie. I'm a client."

"*What* is going on?"

"Lawyer-client confidentiality. Say it."

"Lawyer-client confidentiality," Katie parroted with exasperation.

"I think Sagittarius Eclipse is involved in an embezzlement scheme against Ryder International."

"Montana." Katie drew out the word in a triumphant voice, obviously making the connection with Amber's father's business.

Fine by Amber, she'd rather have Katie connecting her to Jared Ryder than to Royce. Even thinking his name brought up an image of last night, and Amber was forced to shake it away in order to concentrate.

"You going into my line of work?" asked Katie.

Creighton Waverley Security was famous in Chicago for specializing in corporate espionage, and they'd investigated plenty of other corporate crimes along the way.

"Just for the week." Though Amber could already see the appeal of the profession. The harder she looked for information, the more involved she became in the hunt.

"You looking for anything specific?"

"A bank account. A name. A guy named McQuestin might be involved."

Although Royce was sure McQuestin was honest, Amber wasn't prepared to rule anything out. She'd looked back as far as she could in the financial records this morning, and Sagittarius Eclipse had received millions over the years. Maybe McQuestin hadn't even broken his leg. Maybe he was on his way to some offshore haven even now.

"I'll see what I can find. And, Amber?"

"Yes?"

"You serious about this breakup?"

Amber didn't hesitate. "Yes."

"Why?"

Good question. Hard to put into words. "He's just not the right guy for me."

Katie's accusing tone was back. "When did he become not the right guy for you?"

"Katie."

"When he made his first million? When he bought you a three-carat diamond? When he received the party nod for the nomination? Or when he planned the honeymoon to Tahiti?"

"Hargrove planned a honeymoon to Tahiti?" It was the first Amber had heard about it.

"Yes! Just last night he was showing me some—"

"You saw Hargrove last night?"

There was a small pause. "He was desperate, Amber. He needed a date for that hospital thing with the Myers."

"You went on a date with Hargrove?"

"Of *course* not." But there was something in Katie's tone. "He couldn't show up stag, and I've met Belinda Myers before, so…"

Amber rolled the image of Katie and Hargrove around in her head. No problem for her. She really didn't care. "Did you have a good time?" she asked.

"That's not the point."

Royce appeared in Amber's peripheral vision, on

horseback, moving along the river trail between the staff cabins and the barbecue setup. Even at this distance, the sight of him took her breath away.

"Gotta go," she said to Katie. "Call me as soon as you find something."

"Uh… Okay, sure."

"Thanks, Katie. I miss you." Amber quickly signed off.

Royce spotted her, and the sizzle of his gaze shot right to her toes. He turned his horse toward the house, and she headed for the deck's staircase.

Glances and brief, public conversations were all Royce had managed to share with Amber throughout the day. So he was disappointed when he finally found her up at the jumping-horse outfit, and she was sitting on the front porch laughing with his sister and another man.

As he exited the pickup truck, Royce's first thought was that Hargrove had found her. The idea tightened his gut and sped up his stride. She certainly seemed happy to see this guy. She was listening to him with rapt attention, smiling, even laughing.

"Royce," Stephanie sang out as his boot hit the bottom stair. Amber glanced up, and the stranger twisted his head.

Royce immediately realized the man was too young to be Hargrove. Plus, he was wearing jumping clothes, not a business suit.

"Wesley, this is my brother, Royce. Wesley is our newest student. He was nationally ranked as a junior."

The young man stood up as Royce trotted up the remaining stairs.

"Good to meet you," Royce said with a hearty

handshake, ignoring how relieved he felt that the guy wasn't Hargrove. Wesley looked to be about twenty-one. Not much younger than Stephanie and Amber, but no immediate competition.

"You, too." Wesley nodded. "I'm honored to be working with Stephanie."

Royce smirked at his sister. "Well, we'll see how honored you feel a month from now."

"Hey," she protested, reaching out to swat his arm.

"Can I grab you a beer?" Wesley offered, nodding to a cooler against the wall. "I picked up a dozen at a microbrewery in San Diego."

"Thanks," Royce agreed, and the younger man headed for the far side of the porch.

"I've got something for you," Amber stage-whispered, and Royce's attention shot immediately to her dancing eyes.

His chest tightened, and he wondered if she was going to proposition him right here in front of Stephanie. Not that it would be a bad thing. They'd seemed to come to a tacit agreement to keep their relationship secret. But there was no real reason to do that. They were both adults. She'd officially broken off her engagement. They were entitled to date each other if they wanted.

"Sagittarius Eclipse," she said, and he realized his brain had gone completely off on the wrong track. "I have a name."

"Yeah?" He pushed an empty deck chair into the circle.

"Norman Stanton."

Royce froze, brain scrambling while Amber kept talking.

"He's an American, originally from the Pacific North—"

"Later," Royce barked.

Amber drew back, squinting at his expression.

He moderated his voice, forcing a smile when he realized Stephanie was staring at him in confusion. "I want to hear how things are coming with the barbecue."

Then he nodded to Wesley as he returned with the beer. "Thanks," he told him. "So, are you training for any competition in particular?"

Out of the corner of his eye, he could see that Amber was confused, probably hurt, but there was nothing he could do about that at the moment. He pretended to listen to Wesley's answer, while his mind reeled.

Stanton. Damn it. A name out of his worst nightmare. After all these years, they were being blackmailed by a Stanton?

How much did the bastard know? How long had he known it? And why the hell hadn't his grandfather or McQuestin told him before now?

Eight

Amber waited until they'd passed the lights of Stephanie's yard and were headed down the dark, ranch driveway before turning to Royce in the pickup truck. "What did I do?"

"Nothing." But his answer was terse, and she could tell he was upset. Their speed was increasing on the bumpy road, and she gripped the armrest to stabilize herself.

"I don't understand. It's good information. I don't know if you realize how hard I had to dig—"

"Where did you get it? Where did you come up with the name Stanton?"

"Katie found a bank account in the Cayman Islands."

Royce hit her with a hard glance, staring a bit too long for safety. "Who's Katie?"

"Watch the road," she admonished as a curve rushed up at them in the headlights.

He glanced back, but only long enough to crank the wheel. "Who is Katie?"

"She's my best friend, my maid of honor."

"I thought you weren't getting married."

"I'm *not* getting married." Amber took a breath. "She would have been my maid of honor. She's a lawyer. Her firm specializes in corporate espionage, but they investigate all kinds of criminal activity."

Royce's voice went dark. "McQuestin is not a criminal."

"I never said he was."

"You had no right to disparage a man's name—"

"I didn't disparage anything. Katie's my friend. She works for Creighton Waverley Security, and she's our lawyer now. Everything she finds out is confidential."

Royce didn't answer, but she could almost hear his teeth gritting above the roar of the engine and the creak of the steel frame as the truck took pothole after pothole.

"Who is Stanton?" she dared.

His hands tightened on the steering wheel, face stony in the dim dashboard lights. "Nobody you need to worry about."

Something inside Amber shriveled tight. She'd felt so close to Royce last night. Between lovemaking, they'd shared whispered stories, opinions, worldviews. She'd thought they were becoming friends.

"I have more," she told him, not above bribery.

"What else?"

She crossed her arms over her chest. "Who's Stanton?"

Royce glared at her. It was the first time she'd had his true anger directed at her. But she stiffened her spine. "Who is Stanton?"

"Forget it."

"*Why?* Why won't you let me help you?"

He geared down for a hill. "There are things you don't understand."

"No kidding."

"No offence, Amber. But I barely know you."

"No offence, Royce. But you've seen me naked."

"And that's relevant how?"

"I'm just saying—"

"That it's not about to happen again unless I talk?"

"You think I'd use sex to bribe you?"

He let go of the steering wheel long enough for a jerking hand gesture of frustration. "Why do you jump to the absolute *worst* interpretation?"

"I'm trying to understand you."

"Well, I'm not having the slightest success understanding you." He sucked in a deep breath.

She let a few beats go by in silence, forcing herself to calm down. In her mind, this argument was completely separate from any future sexual relationship. She moderated her voice. "Maybe if you told me what was going on."

"Maybe if you let me keep my private business private."

Okay, now that crack would probably impact on their future sexual relationship.

"Fine," she huffed. "There's this numbered holding company." She pulled a note from her pocket and checked it in the dim light. "One-four-nine-five-eight, twelve-zero-ninety-three is registered in Liechtenstein with bank accounts in Liechtenstein, Switzerland and Grand Cayman. Its only asset is a company called Eastern Exploration Holdings. Eastern Exploration owns several parcels of property, mostly in the Bahamas. It also owns one company, Sagittarius Eclipse. One-four-nine-five-eight, twelve-zero-ninety-three is solely owned by Norman Stanton."

The truck rocked to a halt in front of the ranch house.

"His last known address was in Boston, Massachusetts," Amber finished.

Royce killed the lights and turned the key, shutting down the engine. "You don't know where he is now?"

"Not yet." She yanked up on the door handle, and the door creaked wide.

"But you're looking?" Royce followed suit.

"We're looking," said Amber, sliding off the high bench seat and onto the dirt driveway. She'd taken to wearing a pair of tattered, flat, canvas runners she'd found in a closet by the back door. They weren't as sturdy as the cowboy boots favored by everyone else, but they beat the heck out of the high heels she'd arrived in.

"How long will it take?" he asked as they headed for the porch.

"I don't know." Her voice was still testy.

Royce frowned at her.

"It'll take as long as it takes. He could be hiding. He might have left the country." She headed up the stairs. "Maybe someone warned him McQuestin was hurt, and he's worried he'll get caught."

"Who would warn him McQuestin was hurt?"

Amber paused at the front door. "Maybe McQuestin."

Royce turned the knob and shoved open the door. "McQuestin wouldn't do that."

She walked inside. "You're putting a lot of faith in a man who's been authorizing secret payments."

"He has his reasons." The door slammed shut, and Royce moved up close.

Amber turned, then drew back from the intensity in his eyes.

He moved closer.

She stepped back again, coming up against the wall in the foyer.

He braced a hand on either side of her, dipping his head.

"Royce?"

"Yeah?" He kissed her, and her protest was muffled against his mouth.

He kissed her again, softer, deeper, and a flame of desire curled to life in the pit of her belly.

His hands cupped her chin, deepening the kiss, pressing his strong body flush against hers, evoking near-blinding memories of the night before.

"What are you doing?" she finally gasped.

"It's not obvious?" There was a thread of laughter deep in his throat, his warm breath puffing against her skin.

"No."

"Makeup sex."

"But I'm still mad at you."

"You are?" He feigned surprise as he kissed her neck, her collarbone, her shoulder. He found the strip of bare skin at the top of her jeans, skimming his knuckles across her navel. "Then let's see what we can do to change that."

* * *

Royce feathered his fingertips across Amber's stomach, the narrowing at her waist, the indentation of her navel and the small curve of her belly. Her skin was pale and supple, a light tan line at bikini level, barely above where the sheet covered her legs.

She was by far the most beautiful woman he'd ever seen. Her blond hair, mussed at the moment, was thick and lustrous, reflecting the pink rays of the rising sun. Her eyes were deep blue, a midsummer sky right now, but they'd been jewel bright last night while they made love. Her lips were full, deep red and tempting.

Even her ears were gorgeous, delicate and small, while her neck was graceful, her shoulders smooth, and her breasts were something out of his deepest fantasy. Add to that her quick wit, her intelligence and her sense of fun, and she was somebody he could keep in his bed for days on end.

He'd had sex with plenty of women over the years, slept with only some of them, ate breakfast with fewer still. And in all that time, he'd never had an urge to bare his soul to a single one.

Now, he did.

Now, he wanted to tell her anything and everything.

He let his fingers trace the curve of her hip bone, made up his mind and took the plunge. "My father killed a man named Stanton."

Amber's head turned sharply on the stark white pillow. "He what?"

"Killed him," Royce repeated, hand stilling, cupping her hip.

"Was it an accident?"

"Nope."

"I don't understand."

"It was on purpose. Frank Stanton was having an affair with my mother."

Amber's eyes widened and she rolled sideways, propping her head on one elbow. "Did they get into a fight?"

"I guess you could say that. My father shot him."

Amber stilled. The sun broke free from the horizon, and the pink rays morphed to white.

"Did your father go to jail?" Her voice was hoarse.

Royce shook his head. "He died that same day."

Amber swallowed. "And your mother?"

"Died with my father. Their truck went off the ranch road in the rain. They both drowned in the river."

"After he shot Stanton."

"I always assumed he panicked." Though Royce had never delved too deeply into his father's possible motivations for speeding down the ranch road with his unfaithful mother. "There was no trial, of course. Everybody chalked the shooting up to a failed robbery, and the accident was ruled just that, an accident. For years, I thought I was the only one who knew the truth."

"How did you know?"

"I found my mother's confession letter."

Amber sighed, eyes going shiny with sympathy. "Oh, Royce."

"I burned the letter, and the secret was safe. But then, on his deathbed, my grandfather Benteen told Jared he'd heard the shot. When my father drove away, Benteen dumped the gun in the river because he didn't want his son tried for murder."

Royce had wished that Jared never found out. But

now it was better that he had. "So, I know, and Gramps knew, and Jared knows." Royce blew out a breath.

"Plus McQuestin," Amber said softly, obviously putting the pieces together. "And somehow Norman Stanton."

"Allowing him to blackmail my family."

She lay back down. "To keep the secret?"

"Our reputation was important to Benteen."

"But, millions of dollars' worth of important?"

Royce had asked himself that same question, and he didn't have a good answer. What the hell were Benteen and McQuestin thinking? His father couldn't be tried. There wasn't a man in the state who'd fault Royce's father for retaliating against Stanton.

That left their mother's reputation. And, as far as Royce was concerned, she'd made her own bed. He couldn't imagine paying millions of dollars protecting a woman who'd betrayed her own family.

Well, from this point on, he and Jared were in charge, and not a single dime of Ryder money was getting into the hands of a Stanton.

"The payments stop now," he vowed to Amber. "And I want to know everything there is to know about Norman Stanton."

She put her hand on Royce's shoulder. "You're not going after revenge, are you?"

He turned his head to look her in the eyes. "I *am* going after my money."

"Royce."

He raised his eyebrows, all but daring her to argue.

She searched his expression. "I don't want you to get yourself in trouble."

His anger switched to resolve, and he couldn't help

but smile. Her sentiment was admirable, but completely unnecessary.

"Darlin'," he told her. "If I was you, I'd be worried about Norman Stanton, not about me."

Six worried Ryder International division heads stared back at Royce around the ranch house dining room table. The doors were closed to the rest of the house, but the windows were open, the happy sounds of an ongoing barbecue and baseball game a jarring counterpoint to the uncomfortable conversation.

If the four men and two women were unsettled by Barry Brewster's firing, they were positively rattled by the potential fallout from the loss of the China deal. Ryder International was a strong company, but it wasn't invincible. They were going to have to take quick and decisive action if they wanted to recover.

Jared was still out of touch, but it didn't take a rocket scientist to figure out the answer. Some of the Ryder companies would need to be sold, perhaps entire divisions, which explained the ashen faces around the table. Nobody wanted to be the sacrificial lamb.

"Construction is the bread and butter of the company," Konrad Klaus opened the conversation. He was out-front and aggressive as always. As the head of the largest and longest-standing division of the corporation, he wielded considerable influence with his counterparts.

"It's pretty shortsighted to mess with high tech," Carmen Volle put in.

Mel Casper threw down his pen. "Oh, sure. Everybody look at sports and culture. It's not always the bottom line, you know. We're carrying the marketing load for everybody else."

Royce cut them all off. "This isn't divide and conquer," he warned. "Jared's not coming back to a war. I've got your reports—"

"We wrote those before we had the facts," said Konrad.

Konrad's respect factor for Royce had never been high. But it was rare that it mattered. It mattered today.

Royce gave him a level look. "Precisely why I asked for them up front. I wanted the facts, not half a dozen individual lobbying efforts."

"So you can pick us off like fattened ducks?" asked Mel.

"*That's* the attitude you want to project?" Royce needed loyalty and teamwork right now. He wasn't looking to get rid of anybody else, but he wasn't looking to babysit any prima donnas, either.

"I say we wait for Jared to get back," said Konrad.

Royce turned to stare the man down. "What part of fifty million dollars didn't you understand?

Konrad glowered but didn't answer.

"We start today," said Royce. He might not be as involved in the operations of Ryder International as Jared, but he was still an owner, and he'd had about enough of people assuming he could be marginalized.

Barry Brewster would never have treated Melissa the way he'd treated Amber. Just because Royce flew a jet didn't mean he was incapable of anything else. Starting here and now, he was taking a stand—both with Norman Stanton, and with the brass at Ryder International.

"I don't see how we do that." Konrad tossed out a direct challenge to Royce's leadership.

"Did this company turn into a democracy when I wasn't looking?" Royce asked softly.

"Our loyalty is to Jared."

"Your loyalty should be to Ryder International."

Konrad compressed his lips. The rest of the division heads looked down at the table. Royce realized it was now or never. He had to firmly pick up the corporate reins.

"I'm hiring an expert to do a review," he announced, having made a split-second decision.

The group exchanged dubious glances, but nobody said anything.

"Creighton Waverley Security."

"You think we're criminals?" Konrad thundered across the table.

"I think they're one hell of a research firm," Royce countered calmly. "We're going to review every company we own, take stock and make our decisions. Anybody who's not on board with it is free to leave."

He looked to each of the people in turn around the table. Nobody was happy, but nobody was walking away, either.

Now that he'd taken the first step on the fly, he supposed the second step had better be to have Amber put him in touch with her best friend's firm.

Amber helped a waiting group of children into the back of the wooden wagon, while a Ryder cowboy double-checked the harnesses on the matched Clydesdale team out front. Sasha was handing out giant chocolate chip cookies while, off to one side, Wesley was teasing Stephanie with his lariat. Amber did a double take of the two. If she wasn't mistaken, Wesley had developed a crush on his riding instructor.

She smiled to herself. Wesley was a very attractive,

fun-loving man. It wouldn't surprise her in the least if the crush was reciprocated.

"I have to talk to you." The mere sound of Royce's voice behind her caused a little thrill to zip through Amber's body. But in contrast to Wesley, Royce sounded tense and serious.

"Something wrong?" She helped the last little boy into the wagon, dusting her hands off on the sides of her jeans.

Royce moved to the corner of the wagon and pushed up the tailgate, sliding the latch to keep everyone safely inside.

Stephanie planted a foot on the wagon wheel and jumped in with the kids. Wesley quickly followed suit, taking a seat next to her on one of the padded benches, and Amber was sure she'd guessed right.

Royce backed out of the way, towing Amber with him as a cowboy unhitched the lead horse and turned the team toward the road.

"I've been meeting with the division heads," said Royce.

"What did you find out?" Amber had realized Royce and the senior managers were missing, and she'd easily guessed they were talking business. She raised her hand to wave to the cheering children as the wagon creaked down the road.

Royce pulled her toward the shadow of the barn, speaking low into her ear, his voice bringing flash memories of their night together. "I was wondering if you could do something for me."

"I don't know, Royce." She glanced around at the crowds. "There's an awful lot of people in the barn right now."

"You have a one-track mind," he admonished.

She grinned at him. She did seem particularly obsessed with making love.

"Not that I'd say no to a more interesting offer," he clarified. "But I was hoping to get in touch with your friend Katie. I need to know the who's who of Creighton Waverley."

The request brought Amber back to reality. "I thought you were going to let *me* investigate Norman Stanton."

"What?"

"I'm doing a good job," she informed him, pursing her lips.

Royce suddenly grinned.

"What?"

"You. Jumping to conclusions."

"Quit laughing at me."

"Then stop being so entertaining."

"Stop being condescending."

"Stop pouting."

"I like investigating. I want to see this through."

Royce's smile turned sly, and he cocked his head meaningfully toward the barn. "Yeah?" he drawled.

"Now who's got a one-track mind?"

"Guilty," he agreed with an easy smile, but at the same time, he backed off.

A cheer went up at the baseball game, while a freshening breeze brought the aroma of hamburgers from the cook tent.

Amber brushed at a lazy fly.

"I'm commissioning a review of all the Ryder companies," said Royce. "We're going to have to make some tough decisions, and I thought Creighton Waverley might be able to help."

"So, I'm keeping my job?"

He brushed the back of his hand along her upper arm and leaned closer again. "Now *that* remains to be seen."

"I'm not bribing you with sex."

He exaggerated an offended tone. "I'd bribe you with sex."

She extracted her cell phone from her jeans pocket. "I'm bribing you with Katie's phone number."

"Fair enough. I'll bribe you for something else later."

Amber couldn't help but smile as she punched in Katie's cell number.

"Amber," came the breathless answer. "I was just about to call you. Are you at a hoedown or something?"

Amber glanced around for the source of a noise that might have made it through the phone. "What makes you ask that?"

"Checked tablecloths, cowboy hats, horses."

Amber glanced down at her phone, then put it back to her ear. "Do you have some kind of monitor on me?"

"No, I have a white Lexus, over in front of the house. At least I think it's the house. The building with the porch and, yep, it's a hitching rail."

Amber whirled around.

Sure enough, Katie was emerging from a low-slung sports car, wearing a short, blue, clingy dress, high-heeled pumps, with her honey-blond hair in a jaunty updo. Her small bag was beaded, and she reminded Amber of how long it had been since she'd had a manicure or a facial.

Amber took a reflexive step away from Royce. "What are you *doing* here?"

"I have to talk to you."

"That's what telephones are for." A sudden fear

gripped Amber. "There's nobody with you, is there?" Like Hargrove or her parents.

"Relax," said Katie as she picked her way along the edge of the baseball field. "Your secret is safe." She grinned and gave Amber a wave.

Several dozen cowboys followed her progress.

"That's Katie," Amber told Royce.

"She does know how to make an entrance," he muttered, watching as raptly as anyone else on the ranch.

Amber felt an unwelcome pinch of jealousy.

"Who's that with you?" asked Katie as she drew ever closer.

"Royce Ryder."

"Nice."

Okay, jealousy was silly. Katie was an attractive woman, and Royce was an attractive man. They'd noticed. So what?

"Do you have any idea how far away this place is?" Katie called across the grass, folding her phone closed now that she was in shouting range.

"It's Chicago that's far away," Royce countered. "Montana is right here."

Katie grinned as she stepped up, holding out her perfect, magenta-tipped hand. "Katie Merrick. Creighton Waverley Security." She shook, then opened her purse, dropped the phone inside and extracted a business card, handing it to Royce.

"I was about to call you," said Royce.

"Well, isn't that perfect," Katie returned, glancing around the ranch yard. "Any chance they're serving margaritas at this shindig?"

It was a slow walk back to the ranch house, where

Sasha whipped up a blender of margaritas while Amber, Royce and Katie settled in on the deck. Gopher immediately jumped into Amber's lap.

"You'll want Alec Creighton's help," said Katie. She'd been all business while Royce had explained his plans for Ryder International.

"Your boss?" asked Royce as he poured the frozen green concoction into tall glasses.

"My boss's son. He's not with Creighton Waverley. He's sort of a lone-wolf troubleshooter. We subcontract to him on occasion. I can give you a list of a hundred satisfied clients if you like." Katie accepted the drink with a nod of thanks.

"How do I get hold of him?" Royce handed Amber a drink. She still couldn't believe Katie had come all the way to Montana. And since they'd done nothing but discuss Ryder International business since she'd arrived, Amber couldn't begin to guess *why* she'd come all the way to Montana.

"I'll get him to call you." Katie took a sip of her drink. "He won't take on a client without a referral."

"Appreciate that," said Royce with a salute of his drink.

Amber couldn't keep quiet any longer, and her voice came out more demanding than she'd intended. "What are you doing here, Katie?"

Katie shrugged. "I missed you."

It didn't ring true. There was something in Katie's eyes—guilt, maybe fear.

Amber was suspicious. "Did you tell my parents I was here?"

"I can't believe you'd even ask me that. Can't a girl visit her best friend?" Katie took another swig, smiling far too brightly. "Okay if I stay over tonight?"

Nine

Wrapped in a fluffy robe, Katie sat cross-legged on the end of Amber's bed while Amber washed her face at the sink inside the en-suite bathroom door.

"Just how long are you planning to stay here?" Katie asked, her voice muffled by the gush of the running water.

"I haven't decided," Amber answered, dipping her face forward to rinse it, then blindly grabbing for a towel.

As the days went by, she thought less and less about going home. Oh, she knew she'd have to, and probably soon. But there simply wasn't anything tugging her in that direction.

"You know the wedding shower's coming up, right?"

Amber peeked out from behind the towel. "Nobody canceled it?"

"Nobody believed you were serious. There are people flying in from all over the country."

Amber tossed the towel over the rack and paced back into the room. "They're still putting on my wedding shower?"

Katie nodded, while Amber dropped down onto the bed.

"The shower cake's gorgeous," Katie offered.

"This is a disaster."

Katie reached out to rub Amber's arm. "You breaking it off with Hargrove was the disaster. The shower, the dress..." Her hand gripped on Amber's shoulder. Then she abruptly stood up and crossed the room.

"I tried on your dress," she blurted out, turning to brace her back against the bureau.

Amber blinked in surprise. "You did? How'd it look?"

"Gorgeous. Absolutely, stunningly gorgeous."

"It's too bad we'll have to sell it," said Amber. "I can't see ever wearing it."

Katie nodded, her eyes staring blankly into space. "Gorgeous. Really gorgeous."

Amber pictured her friend twirling in front of the mirror. Katie always did have a romantic streak.

Suddenly, Katie clenched her fists, and her eyes scrunched shut. "Oooh, you have to promise me you won't get mad."

"Why would I get mad?" Truth was, Amber wondered if Katie had taken pictures while she modeled the dress. It might be interesting to see how it had turned out.

"I...did something," Katie confessed in a harsh whisper.

"To the dress?"

Katie didn't answer, but the color drained from her face.

"Did you spill something on it? Tear it?" Amber waited for an emotional reaction to her wedding dress being ruined, but it didn't come.

Katie emphatically shook her head. "No. The dress is fine."

"Then what are you so worried about?"

Katie picked up a china horse figurine from the top of the bureau, stroking her fingertip across its glossy surface. She looked at Amber then drew a breath.

"Katie?"

"He saw me in it."

"Who saw you in what?"

"Hargrove. He saw me in the wedding dress."

Amber didn't exactly understand why that was a problem.

Katie set down the figurine, her words speeding up, hands clasping together. "After it was delivered, and I had it on and was prancing around my apartment, he knocked on the door. I didn't know it was him. And, well, when I opened it…" She stopped talking.

"That's when Hargrove saw you in the wedding dress?"

Katie nodded miserably.

Amber fought an urge to smile. "I don't think that's bad luck or anything."

"I'm not so sure."

"Seriously, Katie. I can imagine he was annoyed." Hargrove was nothing if not mired in propriety. "But we're selling the damn thing anyway."

Katie drew a deep breath and squared her shoulders. "Thing is, he really, uh, liked the dress."

"Well, at that price, he'd better have liked it."

"I mean, well…" Katie gazed down at her front, picking a dark speck from the terry-cloth pile of the robe. "He really liked *me* in it."

Amber blinked. "So?" It was probably a good fit. She and Katie were pretty close to the same size.

"And—" Katie buried her face in her hands "—turns out, he liked me out of it, too."

Amber was silent for a full ten seconds. "You're going to have to repeat that."

Katie spread her fingers, peeking out as if she was looking at a horror movie. "I am the *worst* friend *ever.*"

Amber gave her head a little shake. "What are you saying?"

Katie just stared at her.

"Are you saying you *slept* with Hargrove?" It wasn't possible. Nothing made less sense than that.

But Katie nodded. "It happened so fast. One minute he was staring at me. Then he was kissing me. Then the dress came off, and well, yeah, there might have been a bit of a tear around the buttonholes—"

Amber shook her head. "You're not making any sense."

"I am *so* sorry," Katie wailed, pressing a fist against her mouth. "You must hate me."

"No. No, it's not that."

"I had to come and tell you in person."

"I'm confused, not mad." Amber tried to make her point. "Hargrove doesn't get overcome with passion and tear off dresses." Not the Hargrove she knew.

Katie blinked like an owl.

"He's staid, proper, *controlled.*"

Katie blinked once more. A flush rose up from the base of her throat, coloring her face. "Actually…"

Amber rose from the bed. "Actually, what?"

"Sexually speaking, I wouldn't call him staid, and I definitely wouldn't call him proper."

"Are you telling me…?"

Katie gave a meaningful nod.

"You had wild, impulsive sex with Hargrove?"

Something deep and warm flared in Katie's eyes, and she nodded.

"And…it was…*good?*" Amber asked in disbelief.

"It was fantastic."

Amber tried to wrap her head around that. "But… What…" She gripped the bedpost to steady herself. "Sorry. We can't get technical about this." She paused. "Can we?"

Katie cocked her head. "I take it it wasn't always good for you?"

"It was, um…" How did she say this? "Kind of boring."

"No way. You mean he didn't—" Katie's blush deepened.

Amber was forced to stifle a laugh. "Whatever it is you're not saying, I'm pretty sure he didn't do it with me."

Katie fought a grin and lost. "So, you're not mad?"

Amber shook her head, sitting back down on the bed. "I broke up with him."

Katie crossed the room to sit beside her, relieved amusement coloring her tone. "You're probably not going to want the wedding dress back."

"Keep it. Maybe you should keep Hargrove, too. Think of them as a set."

"Maybe I will," Katie said softly.

Amber turned to gaze at her friend and saw the glow in Katie's eyes. She raised her brows in a question, and Katie nodded, wiping a single tear with the back of her hand.

Surprised, but not the least bit unhappy, Amber wrapped her arm around Katie's shoulders. "You do realize what this means, don't you?"

"What?"

"I get to wear the maid of honor's dress." Amber paused. "You know, I always liked that one better anyway."

"Take it," said Katie. "It's yours."

Amber drew a deep sigh. "Wow. Does Hargrove know?"

"That I slept with him?" There was a strengthening thread of laughter in Katie's voice.

"That you came here to confess."

Katie shook her head. "He thinks... Wait. I almost forgot." She bounced off the bed to her small suitcase. "I found something for you."

Hunting through her things, she extracted a manila envelope. "Pictures of Norman Stanton. And his brother, Frank. Also a sister and parents—the three of them died quite a few years back."

Amber accepted the envelope, her thoughts going to Royce. Now it was her turn to feel guilty.

"What?" Katie asked, gauging Amber's expression.

"There's something you don't know."

"About the investigation?"

Amber shook her head. "About me." She shut her eyes for a second. "Oh, hell. I'm sleeping with Royce."

Katie drew back. "Whoa. You cheated on Hargrove?"

"No." Amber swatted Katie with the envelope. "I did not cheat on Hargrove. I broke up with Hargrove. Lucky for you."

"True," Katie agreed. Then she sobered. "This cowboy dude? He rocks your world?"

"And how."

"So." Katie cocked her head toward the bedroom door. "What are you waiting for?"

"I didn't want to be rude."

"Unlike me who slept with your fiancé."

"Ex."

"Whatever. Go see your cowboy. I'll catch you at breakfast."

"You sure?"

"Of course I'm sure. *I* don't want to sleep with you."

Amber grinned, came to her feet and headed out the door.

On the way across the hall, she slit the envelope open, sliding out some eight-by-ten photos.

First one was labeled Norman. He had receding hair, dark, beady eyes and a little goatee. Yeah, she could see him as a blackmailer.

The next was Frank, an older picture. This was the guy who'd broken up Royce's family. He wasn't bad-looking, but not fantastic, either. He seemed a little on the thin side. But maybe that was a generational thing.

She flipped to the next picture, raising her hand to rap on Royce's door. But she froze, hand in midair, the picture of Frank and Norman's sister stopping her cold.

The young girl had a trophy in her hand and a broad smile on her face. Amber stared for a long minute, then slowly turned to the next picture. It was the parents, and the next one was a thirty-year-old family portrait. The final picture was another headshot of Norman.

Amber paged back to the picture of the sister for a final look. Then, stomach twisting around nothing, she rapped on Royce's bedroom door.

His voice was muffled and incomprehensible, but she opened the door anyway. He was lying in bed, a hardcover book in his hands, the bedside lamp glowing yellow against his natural wood walls.

"Hey." He smiled, letting the book fall to his lap.

"Hi." She clicked the door shut behind her.

"Something wrong?"

She nodded.

His smile immediately faded. "Katie?"

"Kind of." Amber moved across the room.

His eyes cooled. "News from…home?"

Amber sat down on the bed. "We have a problem."

He tossed the book aside. "You're reconciling with Hargrove."

"What? *No.* How could you say that?"

Royce didn't answer.

"This has nothing to do with Hargrove." She wanted to be annoyed with Royce for even thinking that it might have been Hargrove, but there wasn't time for that. Instead, she covered his hand, trying to prepare him. "I have pictures of the Stantons. And it's not what we think."

"What do we think?"

She slipped the pictures out of the envelope and spread them on the bed. "Look."

Royce clenched his jaw as he leafed through them. "I've seen Frank Stanton before. He lived on the ranch for a while. Worked with the horses. That's how they met."

"Look at the sister," Amber whispered.

Royce shifted his gaze. "She was into horses, too," he surmised. The trophy was obviously equestrian.

"Look at her chin," said Amber. "Her eyes, the hairline."

Royce glanced from the picture to Amber, brows furrowing.

"Stephanie, Royce."

"What about Stephanie?"

"Stephanie is the spitting image of…" Amber flipped the picture over to read the handwriting on the back. "Clara Stanton, Frank and Norman's sister."

"No." He glanced back down. "She doesn't look anything like…" Royce's breathing went deep.

"He's not blackmailing you over murder."

"Son of a bitch."

She didn't want to say it out loud.

"Son of a bitch!"

"Shh."

Royce turned to her with haunted eyes. "This can't be right."

There was nothing she could say to cushion the blow.

"It can't be real."

It was real all right. Stephanie was Frank Stanton's daughter.

"Who else knows?" he demanded.

"No one."

"Katie?"

Amber shook her head. "Not even Katie. I only figured it out in the hallway thirty seconds ago."

He glanced back down at the picture. "We can't tell Stephanie. It'll kill her. She was two years old when they died. She doesn't even know about the affair."

"I won't tell Stephanie." But Amber realized that meant paying off Norman again.

Royce rolled out of bed, pacing across the floor, photo still gripped in his hand. He was stark naked, but the fact didn't seem to register.

He strode past the bay window, raking a hand through his hair. "We…"

Then he turned at the wall, glanced at the picture and threw it down on a dresser. "I…"

He stopped dead, fisted both hands and glared at Amber. "There's got to be a way out."

"I'm sure there is," she agreed in the most soothing voice she could muster.

He crossed back over to the bed, sat down and uttered a crude cuss. "That bastard's got us by the balls."

Amber didn't know how to answer. It was true, but agreeing seemed counterproductive.

"We can't tell Stephanie," he reaffirmed.

Amber nodded.

Royce snagged his phone from the table. He punched a couple of numbers and put it to his ear.

"Who—" Amber stopped herself.

"Jared."

She knew Jared had been out of touch for several days now.

It appeared he still was.

Royce's voice was terse as he left the voice-mail message. "Jared. Royce. Call me now. Right now." He punched the off button then leaned back against the headboard.

She dared to reach out and touch his bare shoulder. It was hot, hard as a rock. "Anything I can do?"

"Short of fixing a deal with the Chinese, finding a sailboat in the middle of the South Pacific or giving Norman Stanton a fatal disease? Not really."

"Right." She slipped across the bed to sit close beside him, curling her arm around his tense back. "Moral support doesn't really cut it at the moment, does it?"

He wrapped one of his arms around her and then the other. Then he bent to kiss the top of her head. "Moral support is better than nothing."

She struggled to find a smile. "That's always been a dream of mine. To be better than nothing."

He gave her a gentle squeeze and whispered above her head. "Will you stay?"

She nodded against his neck, knowing she was falling fast and hard. His troubles were her troubles, and she'd be by his side just as long as he needed her.

In the morning, when Katie asked for a tour of Stephanie's jumping ranch, Royce resisted the temptation to tag along. Much as he'd love to spend the time with Amber, he was afraid he'd end up studying his sister's expressions, movements and mannerisms for traces of the man he'd hated for twenty long years.

She was still his baby sister. He loved her, and he'd move heaven and earth to protect her. But he needed some time to come to terms with the knowledge she was also Frank Stanton's daughter.

What the hell had his mother been thinking?

Had she known which man fathered Stephanie? What

was her plan? Was she going to take Stephanie with her and Stanton? Would she have destroyed that many lives for her own selfish happiness?

The knowledge crept like a cold snake into his belly.

He smacked open the front door, marching onto the porch to take a deep breath of fresh air. He didn't wish anybody dead, not even Frank Stanton. But he wasn't sorry his mother's plan had failed. He couldn't imagine his life without Stephanie.

An engine roared in the distance, dust wafting up at the crest of the drive. Royce squinted against the midmorning sunshine. He knew it was too early for Amber and Katie to return, but he couldn't help hoping.

Amber had been amazing last night. First she'd let him rail in anger. Then she'd offered practical advice. She seemed to have an uncanny knack for knowing when to stay quiet and when to talk. Finally, against all odds, she helped him find a touch of humor in the face of catastrophe.

Afterward, he'd stayed awake for hours, simply holding her in his arms, letting the feel of her body make his troubles seem less daunting.

It was a car that appeared over the rise. A dark sedan, dusty from the long road in, but unmistakably new, and undeniably expensive. The windows were tinted, and the driver moved tentatively around the potholes dotting dirt and sparse gravel.

Not a local, that was for sure.

Royce made his way down the front stairs, wondering if this could be the mysterious Alec Creighton, or perhaps someone from the Ryder Chicago office.

The car eased to a halt. The engine went silent. And the driver's door swung open wide.

Royce didn't recognize the tall man who emerged. He looked to be in his late thirties. He was clean shaven, his hair nearly black. He wore a Savile Row suit and an expensive pair of loafers. His white shirt was pressed, the patterned silk tie classic and understated.

To his credit, he didn't flinch at the dust, simply slammed the car door shut and gave Royce a genuine smile, stepping forward to offer his hand. "Hargrove Alston."

Royce faltered midreach but quickly recovered. "Royce Ryder."

He resisted the urge to grip too hard, though he squared his shoulders and straightened his spine, watching Hargrove's expression closely for signs that there was going to be a fight.

"Good to meet you," Hargrove offered. There wasn't a trace of anger or resentment in the man's eyes. Either he didn't know about Royce and Amber, or the man had one hell of a poker face.

"What brings you to Montana?" Royce opened.

A split second of annoyance narrowed the man's eyes. "For starters, I understand you're harboring my fiancée."

Royce resented the accusation. "It was at her request."

Hargrove's smile flattened. "I'm sure it was. I'd like to speak with her if you don't mind."

"She's not here." The statement was true enough. Amber might be close by, she wasn't specifically on the ranch this very moment.

Hargrove glanced to the house then back to Royce. "You have a reason to lie to me?"

"I have no reason to lie."

Hargrove regarded him with obvious impatience.

"I can try to pass along a message," Royce offered, folding his arms over his chest and planting his feet apart on the dusty drive.

"You do know who I am, right?"

"You said you were Hargrove Alston."

"I'm not accustomed to being stonewalled, Mr. Ryder."

"And I'm not accustomed to uninvited guests on my land, Mr. Alston."

Hargrove's expression went hard. "I know she's here."

"I told you she wasn't."

There was a pause while the entire ranch seemed to hold its breath.

"But you do know where she is."

Royce did. Since he preferred not to lie, he didn't answer.

Hargrove gave a cool, knowing smile. "She does bring out the protective instincts."

The assessment rang true. And it reminded Royce how well Hargrove knew Amber. She had been bringing out Royce's protective instincts from the moment they'd met.

He decided it was time to stop the pretense. "I assume you're here to drag her back to Chicago."

The shot of pain that flitted through Hargrove's eyes was quickly masked by anger. "I'm here to tell her she can't solve her problems by running away from them."

Guilt hit Royce square in the solar plexus. Amber

had, in fact, run away from Hargrove. And Royce had helped her.

His thoughts went to his father, and an unwelcome chill rippled up his spine. His mother had written a letter. Amber had settled for a text.

Not that Royce was anything like Frank Stanton. Looking back to his teenage memories, Frank had deliberately and methodically lured a woman away from her husband and children.

"Do you have any idea why she left?" he found himself asking.

"Only Amber knows the answer to that." Hargrove shook his head in disgust. "Forget that the wedding dress arrived from Paris this week, that the caterer's put the Kobe beef on hold, that the florist has a Holland order in limbo and that the press has been commenting on Amber's absence. We have fifty people arriving for the wedding shower on Saturday. Her mother's frantic with worry."

Royce swallowed, considering for the first time the destruction Amber had left in her wake.

Hargrove's dark eyes glittered. "I can't wait to sit her down and ask a few questions."

"Did you think about canceling everything?" Royce ventured. If it was him, and the bride went AWOL, as Amber had, Royce couldn't see himself waiting around.

"Are you married, Mr. Ryder?"

Royce shook his head.

"Ever been in love?"

"Nope."

"Well, once you get there, you'll find yourself making allowances for the most inappropriate behavior."

"So, you'd take her back?"

"You don't throw this away over some prewedding jitters. Our plans have been in the works for four years. Our relationship is built on mutual goals and respect. And the foundation of my entire campaign has been built around the fresh faces of Mr. and Mrs. Hargrove Alston. If we're lucky, she'll be pregnant by the primaries."

It sounded a little cold-blooded to Royce. But it also sounded as though Amber was fundamentally entwined in Hargrove's life. And he hadn't considered the situation from Hargrove's perspective.

Amber herself had admitted he was a decent guy. He wasn't malicious or abusive. He simply wasn't as exciting as she'd hoped.

Well, hell, honey, it had been four years. When you were in it for the long haul, the thrill of romance eventually turned into the routine of everyday life.

"There's no way you end something like this on a whim," Hargrove finished, and Royce couldn't deny the man's point.

Relationships took work. They took patience and commitment. They didn't need third party interference. An honorable man would have walked away the minute he saw her diamond ring.

And what the hell had Royce expected? Amber wouldn't stick with him any more than she'd stuck with Hargrove. In the end, he would have been left with nothing but a broken heart and the knowledge he'd destroyed another man's life.

Another engine sounded on the driveway. Before the blue pickup even crested the hill, Royce knew exactly who had arrived.

Ten

"You *didn't*," Amber rasped to Katie as the truck rocked to a stop behind Hargrove's car, and the dust cleared around them.

"I really didn't," Katie responded, her face pale.

"Did you talk to him last night?"

"Just about business."

"Did you tell him we were together?" Amber squinted at Hargrove, then at Royce, trying to interpret their posture.

Katie clutched the dashboard. "I hinted we were in Chicago."

"He knew I wasn't in Chicago. He must have tracked you here."

"Damn it," Katie cursed.

"You go talk to him," said Amber.

"No way."

"You're the one who slept with him. Maybe he's here for you."

Katie frantically shook her head. "Neither of us have even mentioned it. He's here for you."

"He doesn't want me."

But Hargrove's accusatory gaze was focused directly on Amber.

"I don't think he knows that," Katie offered.

This time Amber swore between clenched teeth. She grabbed the gearshift, setting up to pull it into Reverse. "I say we run for it."

"I don't think that's an option," Katie ventured, her gaze tracking Royce as he paced toward the truck.

He looked angry.

Had Hargrove been rude?

Royce reached for the handle and swung open her door. "There's somebody here to see you."

"I'm sorry, Royce. I didn't expect—"

"You knew he'd come," said Royce, hand gripping the top of the door frame. "*I* knew he'd come."

Amber had fervently hoped he wouldn't. She glanced at Katie, who sat completely still, eyes front. No help there. Finally, she took a breath and pulled the key from the ignition.

Royce stepped back out of the way, as Hargrove marched up.

"Montana?" Hargrove accused. "Honestly, Amber, could you make things any more difficult?"

Royce backed off farther, and she knew he was leaving.

"Royce, don't—"

But he shook his head, sliding his eyes meaningfully toward Hargrove.

And he was right. They might as well get this conversation over with.

"We need to talk," rasped Hargrove, moving in too close and pushing the truck door closed.

"There's not a lot left to say," she responded, pushing her windblown hair behind her ears and gathering her courage as Royce left.

It was hard for her to imagine what came after *you slept with the bridesmaid, and I fell for someone else.*

"Do you have any idea how much trouble you've caused?" Hargrove growled. "We've got a thousand people working on the wedding. Nobody knows whether to stop, go, or hold."

"I already told you. They can stop."

"You can't just shut this down on a dime, Amber. We had plans. There's the campaign, the press."

"I'm not marrying you to get good press, Hargrove."

He held up his hands in frustration. "This isn't a one-shot article, Amber. We're talking about my entire political career."

"Yours won't be the first high-profile wedding that was canceled."

"And do you *know* what happened to the others?"

"I don't care what happened to the others. I don't love you, Hargrove. And you don't love me."

"That's ridiculous."

"Then why did you sleep with Katie?"

His jaw went taut. "*That* was a mistake."

"Excuse me?" Katie squeaked from beyond the open window, reminding them both of her presence.

Hargrove's nostrils flared.

"A mistake?" Amber scoffed. "What? Did you trip and accidentally tear off the wedding dress?"

"I don't know what she told you."

"I'm right *here*," Katie pointed out, exiting the truck and slamming the passenger door for emphasis.

"She said you were wild with passion."

"That's ridiculous." But a flush rose up his neck.

"You never tore off *my* dress," said Amber.

"That was out of respect."

Amber shook her head at Hargrove. "It was out of disinterest. Admit it."

"I'm not here to fight with you."

"That's good," said Amber as she dared a glance to where Katie was glaring daggers at him. "Because I think I'd have to take a number."

Hargrove glanced at Katie. "Can you give us some privacy."

"No." She stood her ground.

"This isn't about you."

"The hell it isn't."

"*I'm* going to give *you two* some privacy," said Amber.

Hargrove quickly reached for her arm. "Amber—"

"It's over, Hargrove." She backed out of his reach. "I'm truly sorry about the press and the campaign, but I can't marry you."

"Amber!" He looked genuinely fearful. "You don't know what you're doing to me."

She shook her head. "You don't know what you're doing to yourself. Talk to Katie."

"This isn't about Katie."

"It should be." Amber backed up a few more steps. "Don't screw this up, Hargrove," she warned.

Then she turned away, scanning the yard and finding Royce in a round pen, doing groundwork with a black horse.

Heart still pounding, stomach still cramped, she made her way to the rail and leaned over to watch.

Royce shifted his arms, and the horse sped up. Then he slowed it down, turned it and had it trotting in the opposite direction. It was near poetry, and the tension leached out of her body.

Several minutes later, he approached the animal. He stroked its neck, clipping a lead rope to its bridle then tying it to a rail. He walked through the soft dirt toward Amber.

He braced his hands on the opposite side of the fence. "You here to say goodbye?"

She drew back in surprise. "No."

He nodded toward Hargrove. "He came a long way."

"I told you, I'm not marrying him."

"Why not?"

Amber peered at Royce in confusion. "What do you mean why not?" She leaned forward. "I've just spent the last week with you."

He shrugged. "That doesn't mean anything."

She opened her mouth, struggling to form words.

"I'm new, Amber." He stripped off a pair of leather gloves. "I seem interesting and exciting. You're on vacation, having a fling."

Amber's fingertips went to her temple. "A fling?"

He calmly tucked the gloves under his arm and adjusted his Stetson. "Hargrove is willing to take you back. You should seriously consider his offer."

Her frustration was turning to anger. "You said

anybody who told me that was short-sighted and stupid."

"Guess I was wrong."

She shook her head, but he stayed stubbornly silent.

She clenched her jaw, then enunciated her words slowly and carefully. "I do not love Hargrove."

"You don't know that for sure."

"I absolutely know that for sure. Because I love *you*, Royce."

The words went unanswered. But she wasn't sorry. This was no fling. He was falling for her, too. She'd bet her life on it.

No one had ever treated her the way Royce did. He was compassionate, attentive and so very sexy. And she was positive he didn't open up with many other people the way he'd opened up with her. He'd flat out told her nobody else knew about his father. And their lovemaking was off the charts.

He scoffed out a laugh. "You don't love me."

She smacked her hand on the rail in frustration. "What is the matter with you? Are you afraid of Hargrove?"

Royce's eyes glittered. "I'm not afraid of anybody."

"Well, I *know* you feel it, too."

He whipped off his hat, banging it on his thigh to release the dust. "If by *it,* you mean lust, then you're right."

"I don't mean lust."

"People don't fall in love in a week."

"People can fall in love in an hour."

"Not so it lasts." It was his turn to lean in. "It's lust, Amber. It's a fling. What you have with Hargrove is real, and you need to go back to him."

"Hargrove loves Katie."

Royce smacked his hat back on his head. "Then why's he here looking for you?"

"He doesn't know it yet." She realized that sounded lame, but it was completely true. Amber had very high hopes that Hargrove would wake up to the truth about Katie.

"Now you're grasping at straws. Go back to reality, Amber. Get married in that big cathedral and have beautiful babies for the campaign trail."

"Are you *listening* to yourself?" She gripped the rail. "You're willing to throw away everything that's between us?"

A part of her couldn't believe it. A part of her expected to wake up any second. But another brusque, insidious part of her realized she'd made a horrible mistake.

She might have fallen for Royce. But Royce hadn't fallen for her.

"You've spun a nice fantasy, here," he said. Then he nodded toward Hargrove's car. "But your reality is over there."

Her throat closed over, and she swallowed hard. "You're asking me to leave?"

His expression was unreadable. "I'm asking you to leave."

She gave a stiff nod, unable to speak. Royce didn't love her. He didn't want her. And she'd made a complete and total fool of herself.

Two days later, Amber alternated between misery and mortification. Royce might not have loved her, but her heart had fallen hard and fast for him.

It was easy to see what made him such a great pick-up artist. He must make every woman feel loved and cherished—at least temporarily. She wondered about the string of broken hearts he'd left behind.

Then she wondered who he'd be with next. But that thought hurt so much she banished it, blinking back the familiar sting in her eyes as she focused on her mother far across her family's great room.

The replacement-for-the-shower party was in full swing. But Amber didn't feel remotely like celebrating.

Maybe if Royce had simply sweet-talked her into bed, if they'd had fantastic sex, if he'd put her in a cab in the morning, maybe then she could have handled it. But he hadn't simply made love to her. He'd joked and laughed with her, shared his secrets with her, made her feel valuable, important, a part of his world.

"Amber?" Her mother, Reena, approached, concern in her expression.

Amber tried to smile at her mother. Her family had been told that she was the one to break it off with Hargrove. But nobody but Katie knew anything about Royce. Amber planned to keep it that way.

Reena's floor-length chiffon dress rustled to a halt. "Why aren't you visiting, sweetheart?"

"I'm a little tired."

"Are you sure that's all it is?"

"I'm sure." She mustered up a smile.

"That's the best you can do? You look like you're headed for the gallows."

Amber signed. "I'm really not in the mood for a party, Mom."

Reena moved in closer. "But I thought this was what you wanted."

"I didn't want a party."

"Well, you didn't want a shower, either. And the guests were already on their way."

Amber drew a shuddering breath, fighting the tears that were never far from the surface. Emotions alone shouldn't hurt this much. Still, a single teardrop escaped, trailing coolly down her cheek.

"Sweetheart," her mother entreated, drawing Amber close to her side. "Do you miss him so much?"

Amber startled in surprise. How had her mother guessed?

Reena cupped Amber's chin with gentle fingertips, peering deeply into her eyes. "Shall I give Hargrove a call for you? We might be able to talk him into—"

"She's not missing Hargrove," came Katie's voice as she swooped in to join them.

"Of course she is," said Reena. "Just look at her."

"I'm not missing Hargrove," Amber confirmed.

Katie gave Amber a level, challenging look. "She's missing Royce Ryder."

Amber sucked in a gasp.

"Who?" asked her mother, glancing from Amber to Katie and back again.

Katie gave Amber a helpless shrug. "What's the point in hiding it? It's obvious to anyone that you've had your heart broken."

"Who is Royce Ryder?"

"The man she met in Montana."

"I met him at Jared Ryder's wedding," Amber corrected. Where he'd picked her up in the bar for a quick fling. At least that's the way *he* remembered it.

Reena's jaw dropped a notch, and her hand went to her chest. "You were unfaithful to Hargrove?"

"I *wasn't* unfaithful to Hargrove." Frustration finally

gave Amber an emotion to replace despair. "In fact, Hargrove was unfaithful to me." She returned Katie's look. "With *Katie*."

Katie's face went pale, and Reena's jaw dropped another notch.

"They'd already split up," Katie hastened to assure Reena.

"That's true," Amber admitted. "Nobody was unfaithful to anybody."

Katie's voice went soft. "And she did fall in love with Royce."

Amber was too exhausted to deny it.

"Oh, sweetheart." Reena took Amber's hand. Her mother was a romantic to the core. "That terrible man broke your heart?"

"I broke my own heart." As she said the words out loud, Amber admitted to herself they were true. "We barely knew each other. And my expectations were… Well, he's just such an incredible man. You'd love him, Mom. You really would."

Reena's narrow arm curled around her shoulders. "I wouldn't like him at all. He broke my baby's heart."

Jared's familiar voice barked at Royce over the phone. "What the hell did you do?"

"Jared? Finally. Where are—"

"I need an explanation," Jared demanded.

Royce swiveled on the ranch house office chair, assuming Jared had been in contact with the Ryder office in Chicago. "I don't even know where to start."

"Start with how you broke Amber Hutton's heart and infuriated one of our most important clients."

Royce nearly dropped the phone. "Huh?"

"I've only been gone a week, and you screw up this badly."

"She *called* you?" Royce could hardly believe it. What was Amber doing running to Jared?

"David Hutton called me. He's threatening to cancel his lease. You are aware that he's our second-biggest client, right?"

"Don't patronize me."

"Then don't sleep with our clients' daughters."

What could Royce say to that? "It just…happened."

"Right. Well, un-happen it."

"I don't think that's physically possible."

"You know what I mean. Fix it."

"I can't fix it. She's engaged to someone else."

"What?" Jared's voice rose to a roar.

"Hargrove Alston."

"Then why did you sleep with her?"

Royce didn't have an answer for that. There wasn't an excuse in the world for what he'd done.

Jared was silent for a moment. "David thinks she's in love with *you?*"

"I'm not breaking up her engagement."

"Admirable," said Jared.

"Thank you."

"Could've thought of it *before* you slept with her."

Royce grunted.

"So, how're you going to fix it?"

"I'll talk to her."

"What are you going to say?"

"None of your business." Royce didn't have the first clue.

He'd been thinking about it for days, and had come to the conclusion that by bringing Amber to Montana, he'd turned a momentary hesitation into a life-altering event.

Whatever crazy fantasy Amber had spun around Royce wasn't real. She barely knew him. And he barely knew her. If relationships built on years didn't last, there was no hope at all for one that was built on a mere week.

"Make it my business."

"No."

Jared went silent on the other end of the line for a few beats. "You ever think…"

Royce drummed his fingers on the desktop.

"That maybe she's not…"

"Not what?" Did Jared have something intelligent to add here or not?

Jared drew a breath. "I mean, she might really be in love—"

"No!" Royce barked.

"Could happen."

"No, it could not."

"I'm a married man, Royce. And I'm telling you it could happen."

"You've been married a week. Talk to me in twenty years."

"You're going to make a woman wait twenty years?"

Royce felt his frustration level rise. "I'm going to make a woman wait until she's sure."

"How're you going to know that?"

"I'll just know."

"Like you do now?"

"What I know now is that she's taken, and she's

confused, and she has obligations that have nothing to do with me."

"She's not Mom," Jared said softly.

"Don't even go there."

"And you're not Frank Stanton."

"I'm hanging up now."

"Mom and Dad's relationship was demanding and complex. He worked too hard and she had stars in her eyes."

"And you don't think all marriages are demanding and complex?" That was what the long haul was all about. It meant sticking together through the rough times, knowing better times would come again. It didn't mean bailing the second life got a little humdrum.

"Did it ever occur to you that Dad might have shared the blame?"

"He didn't screw around on her," Royce practically shouted.

"Yeah, but he wasn't perfect. He had a temper. Hell, he shot a guy."

"The son of a bitch deserved it. I'd have shot him, too."

"You mean, if he slept with Amber?"

"Hell, yes."

"Gotcha."

Royce went silent, his jaw clamping down.

What had just happened? He was the illicit lover in this triangle, not the betrayed husband.

Jared's voice turned jovial. "Okay, fixing this is going to be way easier than I thought."

"Shut up."

Jared chuckled, and Royce bit down harder on his outrage. His brother could be positively infuriating.

"Let's move on to other problems," he ground out. He wasn't wrong, and Jared wasn't right. And it was definitely time to end this discussion.

His brother's tone changed. "What problems?"

"The China deal fell apart."

"Yeah," Jared sighed. "I was afraid of that."

"We're in a cash crunch because of it. I've got a guy taking a thorough look at our operations. I think we're going to have to streamline."

"He any good?"

"He came highly recommended." Royce drew a breath. "And, Jared. I fired Barry Brewster over China."

"Seriously?"

"He missed the deadline, blew the deal." He'd also insulted Amber, but Royce wasn't going anywhere near that conversation.

"There are a thousand ways to blow a deal with China."

"Yeah, well, he's gone."

"Okay. Your call. You need me to come back early?"

"Let's give it a few more days. There's one more thing…." Royce stopped himself. "You know what? It can wait."

If Jared learned about Norman Stanton and Stephanie, he'd be on the next plane back to the States.

But Royce had already made this month's blackmail payment. Norman Stanton had no idea they were on to him, and there was nothing Jared could do in the short term but worry.

"You sure?" asked Jared.

"I'm sure."

"And fix it with Amber, bro. She's not Mom. You're not Stanton. And everything's a leap of faith."

Amber and Katie stood side by side, gazing into the three-way mirror in Amber's bedroom.

"You don't think it would be too weird?" asked Katie as they admired their reflections in the sleek, sleeveless, pearl-adorned wedding gown and the dramatic oriental silk bridesmaid dress.

"Like I said before," Amber replied. "Think of them as a set. You know I like this one better." She turned and watched the orange, gold and midnight plum shimmer in the sunlight that streamed through her big windows.

"Did I miss something?" came a masculine voice from the doorway.

Amber and Katie whirled simultaneously to see all six foot two of Royce standing in the bedroom doorway. He was wearing a steel-gray business suit, a blue silk tie and a crisp white shirt. His face was freshly shaven, and his blue gaze hungry as he stared at her.

She swallowed the tears that were never far from the surface. His appearance was her dream come true. But she couldn't let herself hope.

"Where did you come from?" asked Katie.

Instead of answering, he strolled into the bedroom, gaze fixed on Amber as he grew closer. "Someone named Rosa said you were trying on your wedding gown."

Amber glanced down at the silk bridesmaid dress. "Something got lost in the translation."

"I was going to rip it from your body." The hunger in his eyes grew more intense.

Amber tipped her head, not sure what to think.

"I flew here at Mach 1," he told her. "All the way

over South Dakota, Iowa and Illinois, I told myself you belonged to Hargrove."

"I don't belong—"

"I told myself I'd reason with you, I'd make you understand you had an obligation to your fiancé, I'd explain again that nobody falls in love in a week, and what you thought you felt for me was an illusion."

He took her hands.

Katie took a few steps toward the door. "Uh, I'm… just going to…" She slipped outside and shut the door behind her.

"At least that's what I told myself," said Royce. "And then Rosa told me you were trying on your wedding dress. And I knew I had to stop you. I knew there was no way I could let you marry someone else."

"I'm not marrying—"

"I still find it impossible to believe a week is any kind of a foundation for a lifelong commitment. I looked up the mathematical odds on marital success. They're not good.

"But I do know I want you. And I know I'll shoot any guy who touches you. And I'm thinking maybe that's a sign that there's something to this."

Amber fought the smile that tightened her lips.

As declarations of love went, this left a whole lot to be desired. But this was Royce, and she knew his demons, and she knew just how difficult it was for him to even contemplate the possibility of happily ever after.

"I love you, Royce."

"You can't know—"

She put her fingertips over his lips. "I do know. And, guess what? I know you love me, too. And I know you're going to figure it out eventually. And if I have to wait a year, or ten or twenty, for you to decide we should stay together, that's fine with me."

His arm snaked around her waist, and he jerked her up tight against him. "I want to start staying together now."

"No problem." She smiled at him, trailing her palms over his chest, wrapping them loosely around his neck. "We'll hang out together while you give this love thing some serious thought."

He settled his other arm around her. "And by hanging out, I hope you mean living together, working together and sleeping together."

"I do," she told him.

"Good." He gave a decisive nod. "Then I'm thinking we'd better be married while we're hanging out. I don't want anyone else to try to steal you. Your father's already a little ticked off at my brother. And there's the whole propriety thing."

"You think it's logical for us to be married while we figure out if we're in love?"

"Completely logical," he said. "Especially if we want a few kids. You're not getting any younger—"

"Hey!" She smacked him on the shoulder.

"And who knows how long it'll take for us to be sure."

"Maybe twenty years?" she asked.

"Maybe even fifty." His expression sobered. His gaze caressed her as he slowly dipped his head. Then his warm, soft lips came down ever so gently onto hers, sealing their bargain.

"What do you say, Amber?" he whispered against her mouth. "Will you spend the next fifty or so years married to me, just in case I love you?"

She nodded, coming up on her bare toes to kiss him again, longer this time, more soundly.

"Yes, I will," she whispered. "Just in case."

His arms engulfed her, and he lifted her completely off the floor. His mouth slanted and his kiss deepened, and she clung to him, heart bursting with joy.

When he finally set her down, slowly sliding her along his body, his grin widened. "Well, what do you know."

"What?"

"I think it might be happening already."

She couldn't help but smile in return. "Imagine that."

He nodded. "And it's really easy. You know, I think I'm going to be very good at this."

"There's not a doubt in my mind."

His blue eyes stared down into hers. "I love you, Amber."

"I know you do, Royce."

"Forever."

"Absolutely."

"Who knew."

"I did."

"You did at that." And he bent to kiss her one more time.

Eleven

Royce couldn't think of a single thing he liked better than the sight of Amber at Hargrove's wedding—wearing the bridesmaid's dress. Katie had been radiant on her walk down the aisle. She'd beamed at Hargrove during the first dance, then laughed with him when they cut the cake. Royce caught the garter again, and this time he knew it was fate.

"She looked spectacular," said Amber as they walked, hand in hand, beneath the lighted tress of the waterfront patio. The reception was in full swing inside the restaurant, notables from both the business and political worlds dancing it up at the black-tie event.

"Your life's not going to be anything like hers," Royce observed, thinking about the reporters hovering in the parking lot.

"No, it's not." Amber grinned, turning to the rail to

stare out across the sparkling water. She took a sip of the bubbly liquid in her champagne flute.

Royce moved up behind her, tracing a fingertip along her bare shoulder. "Any regrets?"

"Yes," she sighed, and he felt a moment's pause.

But she covered his hand with her own, holding his touch against her skin. "I regret saying no to you in the hotel room earlier."

A surge of masculine pride swelled within him, and he leaned down to kiss her shoulder. "I told you so."

"You did."

"Weddings have a way of making women feel all romantic and mushy."

"It's true." She nodded, taking another drink.

"And all those romantic and mushy feelings have a way of turning to—"

"Lust?"

"Which could have been pre-empted," he whispered in her ear. "If you'd only let—"

"There you are, pumpkin," came David Hutton's hearty voice.

Royce immediately stepped back from Amber.

"Seems like I'm always finding you off in a corner with this Ryder fellow at wedding receptions."

"He does have a way of finding me," Amber joked, turning to face her father.

Royce was still a bit jumpy around the man. The two-carat solitaire on Amber's finger had mitigated some of the antagonism, but Royce wasn't sure David had forgiven him for breaking things off with Amber. He also wasn't sure that a jet pilot was an acceptable substitute for a senator as a son-in-law.

"You look amazing," David told his daughter, kissing her gently on the forehead.

"And you look handsome as always," Amber returned.

Royce held out his hand to shake, refusing to let David see anything but confidence. "Good to see you again, sir."

"I trust you'll be making your own wedding plans soon?" David asked him.

"Daddy," Amber admonished.

"Don't want to give the man time to change his mind again."

Royce held the handshake a little longer. "I'm not going to change my mind."

David harrumphed.

"I love your daughter, Mr. Hutton." Royce wrapped an arm around Amber's shoulder and drew her close. "I'm going to marry her and make her happy for the rest of her life."

"I would hope so. What with all the turmoil you caused."

"Daddy, I stopped loving Hargrove before Royce got anywhere near me."

Royce nearly choked on her choice of words. "The wedding will be soon," he assured David.

Amber glanced up at him in surprise. "Royce, we haven't—"

"Very soon." He gave Amber a meaningful squeeze.

David cracked a smile. "You keep my baby girl happy, son. And we'll get along just fine."

"I will," Royce assured the man.

"Call me David."

"Okay."

David winked at Amber and started away. "Don't stay out too late."

"I'm not coming home tonight," she warned him.

David turned his attention to Royce again. "Soon." He waggled a warning finger before he turned away.

"You want to head for Vegas tonight?" Royce asked Amber.

"Vegas is a terrible idea," said Stephanie.

Royce had left the jet under the command of his copilot and dropped into one of the seats in the main passenger cabin.

"Thank you," Amber said to Stephanie from the seat next to him.

They'd picked Stephanie up from a junior jumping show in Denver, and Jared and Melissa were hitching a ride from Chicago to the ranch for the last few days of their honeymoon.

"Well, she'd better come up with something," Royce told his sister. "I don't want her father gunning for me for the next year."

"He likes you," said Amber.

"No, he likes you. He tolerates me because you love me."

"I do love you," she confirmed, giving him a quick kiss on the cheek.

"And I love you," he automatically returned.

"Oh, gag me," Stephanie groaned.

"I thought you were a romantic," Melissa put in, moving up from the back of the cabin where she'd been sitting with Jared.

"I am a romantic. But, yuck, she's kissing my brother."

"Well, I totally get it," said Melissa.

"That's because you kiss my other brother."

Melissa got a gleam in her eyes. "You know what else I do to your other brother?"

Stephanie clapped her hands over her ears. "Pink fuzzy bunnies. Pink fuzzy bunnies."

"What the hell?" asked Royce.

"She's obliterating the image from her brain," Amber informed him.

Royce shook his head at the nonsense. "You," he said to Amber. "Come up with a wedding plan, or we *are* heading for Vegas." Then he exited his seat and moved to the back with his brother.

"Hey." Jared nodded to him, looking up from a table full of reports.

Royce sat down, lowering his voice. "You met with Alec Creighton?"

"I did."

"What did you think?"

Jared glanced to the front of the plane where the three women were chatting. "Seems like a good guy. Smart. On the ball."

"Did you talk to the VPs?"

Jared nodded. "They were shocked about Barry Brewster. It's got them looking over their shoulders. But I think in a good way."

"What about Konrad?"

Jared grinned. "Oh, he really hates you."

"Yeah. I kinda got that."

"He's demanded to deal directly with me from now on. Threatened to quit if you're involved in the construction division."

Royce clamped his jaw, while a burning anger roiled up in his stomach.

"Told him no," Jared said mildly. "Told him you

were taking over the construction division, and if he didn't like it, he should have his letter of resignation on your desk Monday morning."

Royce gaped at his brother. Konrad might be a jerk, but he was an incredibly valuable employee.

"Family is family," said Jared. "It's your company, too, and you did one hell of a job while I was away. Well, except for ticking off David Hutton."

"I'm working on that," said Royce, glancing to Amber, struck as always by how much he adored her.

"That's what counts, bro. Everybody's working hard at head office, looking to streamline, reallocating cash flow. We've survived trouble before."

Royce's attention shifted to his sister, and he lowered his voice. "After that, there's Stephanie."

"Yeah," Jared agreed. "We need to talk about that one."

"Does Melissa know?" asked Royce.

"That Frank Stanton is Stephanie's father?" Jared shook his head. "I'm keeping the club as small as possible for now."

Royce nodded. He was glad Amber already knew; he wouldn't want to have to make the choice to keep a secret from her.

"It was hard enough on me," said Jared. "Finding out what I did the way I did."

Royce nodded his agreement with that, too.

"Stephanie can *never* find out," Jared vowed.

"She won't." Royce had had most of his life to come to terms with his parents' secret, and it had still colored him in ways he hadn't even realized. It had almost cost him the love of his life.

He caught Amber's gaze.

She sobered at the sight of his expression, eyes

narrowing. Then she unobtrusively stood from her seat to move toward him.

He smiled and snagged her wrist, pulling her into his lap to wrap his arms around her.

"What's wrong?" she asked.

"Nothing."

She raised her brows to Jared.

Jared shook his head. "It's all good." His smile was back, and it was easy. "Except *you* can't seem to decide on a wedding."

Royce knew Amber wasn't buying their jovial mood, but she played along. "This is not a decision to take lightly. I'm only getting married once."

"In Vegas," said Royce.

Amber socked him in the arm.

"Tahiti, maybe." Melissa joined in. "On a beach, just family?"

"I vote for Tuscany," Stephanie called out. "Or Paris in the spring."

"She'll be pregnant by spring," said Royce, and Amber gave him a wide-eyed look of surprise.

"And we'd better damned well be married by then," he growled low.

"Babies?" she mused.

"I want babies," he confirmed.

"Good," she whispered and hugged him tightly, pressing her face into the crook of his neck, sighing in contentment, while the rest of his family joked about wedding plans.

Aella closed her eyes and sensed a distinct shift, like movement from the world around her to the unseen world.

She opened her eyes. And had a slight shock at the man standing ten feet away. He wasn't just any man. Her heart leaped and pounded. He reminded her of a fierce warrior from an ancient civilization. Incan? She wasn't sure but she felt his deep power and masculinity.

I'm Aella. Are you the guardian of this sacred site? she asked, hoping her telepathy was strong.

Fox's entire body soared with joy. Fox struggled to put his personal pleasure aside.

Greetings, Aella. I'm the assistant guardian to this sacred area. You may call me Fox. How can I be of service to you, Aella? he asked.

I'm searching for a green sphere. A legend says that the Emperor Pachacuti had seven emerald spheres created for the Emerald Key necklace. He had seven of his priestesses and priests travel the world to hide these spheres from evil forces. It is said that when all seven spheres are found, restrung and worn, that Light will return to the Earth. The fourth sphere is here, at your sacred site. Are you aware of it? Aella held her breath. She loved looking at him, especially his sensual mouth. The desire to kiss him came out of nowhere.

Fox was stunned by the request. *I know of the Emerald Key necklace because I served the emperor at the time it was created. However, I did not realize that one of the spheres is here.*

Aella felt sad. Why? Every time she looked at Fox, her heart felt as if it would tear out of her chest. *May I stay in touch with you as I work with this site?* she asked.

Of course. Fox wanted nothing more than to be here with her. To absorb her ephemeral beauty and hear her speak once more.

Aella's spirit lifted. What *was* this strange connection between them? Her curiosity was strong, but she had more pressing matters. In the next few days, Aella knew her life would change forever. How, she had no idea....

Look for REUNION
by USA TODAY bestselling author
Lindsay McKenna,
available April 2010, only from
Silhouette® Nocturne™.

HARLEQUIN Romance

ROMANCE, RIVALRY
AND A FAMILY REUNITED

THE BRIDES
of
BELLA ROSA

William Valentine and his beloved wife, Lucia, live
a beautiful life together, but when his former love Rosa
and the secret family they had together resurface,
an instant rivalry is formed. Can these families
get through the past and come together as one?

───────────

Step into the world of Bella Rosa
beginning this April with

Beauty and the Reclusive Prince
by

RAYE MORGAN

Eight volumes to collect and treasure!

www.eHarlequin.com

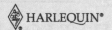
HARLEQUIN®
INTRIGUE®

WILL THIS REUNITED FAMILY
BE STRONG ENOUGH TO EXPOSE
A LURKING KILLER?

FIND OUT IN THIS ALL-NEW
THRILLING TRILOGY FROM TOP
HARLEQUIN INTRIGUE AUTHOR

B.J. DANIELS

WHITEHORSE
MONTANA

Winchester Ranch

GUN-SHY BRIDE—*April 2010*

HITCHED—*May 2010*

TWELVE-GAUGE GUARDIAN—
June 2010

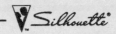

SPECIAL EDITION

**INTRODUCING A BRAND-NEW MINISERIES
FROM *USA TODAY* BESTSELLING AUTHOR**

KASEY MICHAELS

SECOND-CHANCE BRIDAL

At twenty-eight, widowed single mother
Elizabeth Carstairs thinks she's left love behind
forever....until she meets Will Hollingsbrook.
Her sons' new baseball coach is the handsomest
man she's ever seen—and the more time they
spend together, the more undeniable the
connection between them. But can Elizabeth
leave the past behind and open her heart to
a second chance at love?

FIND OUT IN

SUDDENLY A BRIDE

*Available in April
wherever books are sold.*

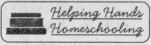

HARLEQUIN *Presents*

2 Stories in 1

HER MEDITERRANEAN PLAYBOY

Sexy and dangerous—he wants you in his bed!

The sky is blue, the azure sea is crashing
against the golden sand and the sun is hot.

The conditions are perfect for
a scorching Mediterranean seduction
from two irresistible untamed playboys!

Indulge your senses with these two delicious stories

A MISTRESS AT
THE ITALIAN'S COMMAND
by *Melanie Milburne*

ITALIAN BOSS,
HOUSEKEEPER MISTRESS
by *Kate Hewitt*

Available April 2010 from Harlequin Presents!

www.eHarlequin.com

HPI2910

REQUEST YOUR FREE BOOKS!

2 FREE NOVELS PLUS 2 FREE GIFTS!

Passionate, Powerful, Provocative!

YES! Please send me 2 FREE Silhouette Desire® novels and my 2 FREE gifts (gifts are worth about $10). After receiving them, if I don't wish to receive any more books, I can return the shipping statement marked "cancel." If I don't cancel, I will receive 6 brand-new novels every month and be billed just $4.05 per book in the U.S. or $4.74 per book in Canada. That's a saving of almost 15% off the cover price! It's quite a bargain! Shipping and handling is just 50¢ per book in the U.S. and 75¢ per book in Canada.* I understand that accepting the 2 free books and gifts places me under no obligation to buy anything. I can always return a shipment and cancel at any time. Even if I never buy another book, the two free books and gifts are mine to keep forever.

225 SDN E39X   326 SDN E4AA

Name	(PLEASE PRINT)	

Address		Apt. #

City	State/Prov.	Zip/Postal Code

Signature (if under 18, a parent or guardian must sign)

Mail to the **Silhouette Reader Service:**

IN U.S.A.: P.O. Box 1867, Buffalo, NY 14240-1867
IN CANADA: P.O. Box 609, Fort Erie, Ontario L2A 5X3

Not valid for current subscribers to Silhouette Desire books.

Want to try two free books from another line?
Call 1-800-873-8635 or visit www.morefreebooks.com.

* Terms and prices subject to change without notice. Prices do not include applicable taxes. N.Y. residents add applicable sales tax. Canadian residents will be charged applicable provincial taxes and GST. Offer not valid in Quebec. This offer is limited to one order per household. All orders subject to approval. Credit or debit balances in a customer's account(s) may be offset by any other outstanding balance owed by or to the customer. Please allow 4 to 6 weeks for delivery. Offer available while quantities last.

Your Privacy: Silhouette Books is committed to protecting your privacy. Our Privacy Policy is available online at www.eHarlequin.com or upon request from the Reader Service. From time to time we make our lists of customers available to reputable third parties who may have a product or service of interest to you. If you would prefer we not share your name and address, please check here. ☐

Help us get it right—We strive for accurate, respectful and relevant communications. To clarify or modify your communication preferences, visit us at www.ReaderService.com/consumerschoice.

SDES10